PORTRAIT OF ROSE

She was young, well-brought up and ingenuous, until circumstances outside her control started her off on an unfortunate path. Thereafter, Rose Delafield seemed to possess no armour against fate. A basic flaw in her character, manifesting itself time and time again, ensured that she was always the loser, despite a few initial years of glamour and excitement preceding the Second World War. Gradually, all that she had come to expect from life proved a chimera.

Yet some intrinsic physical toughness and native wit kept her going, notwithstanding that she was a disaster to herself and all with whom she came into contact. Women—apart from one loyal devotee—shunned her. Men were in turn fascinated and repelled by her. She was aware of this state of affairs but powerless to alter it.

During the war and its aftermath, she became more and more at odds with herself and society. She drifted, like flotsam, searching for an identity which she began associating in her mind with a portrait that was painted of her in 1936 by a famous artist. To trace it became an obsession. She felt it would act as a testimony, a link with the past, when she had been beautiful and desired. But it appeared to be as lost as its sitter.

Portrait of Rose is a powerful haunting story, depicting the inherent frailty of human nature with all its tragic consequences. In it the author has explored new and unusual territory, one in which the reader might well be tempted to say, "There, but the for the grace of God, go I".

PORTRAIT
OF
ROSE

by

Pamela Street

ROBERT HALE · LONDON

©*Pamela Street 1986*
First published in Great Britain 1986

ISBN 0 7090 2766 4

Robert Hale Limited
Clerkenwell House
Clerkenwell Green
London EC1R 0HT

All the characters and incidents
in this book are imaginary
and have no reference to
anyone, living or dead.

Photoset in Plantin by
Kelly Typesetting Limited
Printed in Great Britain by
St Edmundsbury Press
Bury St Edmunds, Suffolk
Bound by Hunter & Foulis Limited

1

At Michaelmas, 1935, a man came to live at Wilcot Grange with a woman who was not his wife. He was called Harvey Frayne. The woman was known as Miss Delafield. Because it was so seldom used, few people thought of her as being the possessor of a rather pretty christian name—Rose—except, perhaps, a servant who chanced to overhear one of the couple's more personal conversations or visitors from London who were staying the weekend. But neither of these eventualities took place very often. Harvey, with his fanatical determination to keep his private life private, saw to that.

At mealtimes, seated one at either end of the long refectory table in the oak-panelled dining-room, the two seemed as remote and formal as the silver-laden expanse of polished wood which divided them. Remarks were confined to the weather, the dogs, the garden, a book or a play, the demise of Ramsay MacDonald's Coalition Government, the forthcoming General Election and the meteoric rise to power of the Nazi party in Germany.

It was the man who initiated each topic, the woman rarely making anything other than perfunctory replies, especially when it came to politics, about which it was obvious she knew nothing. Often, there were quite long silences in the room, broken only by the muted sounds made by Robson, the butler, as he padded to and fro between hotplate and table, waiting on them with an expertise acquired through thirty-seven years' service with the Beresford family, from whom Harvey Frayne had bought—at a knock-down price—Wilcot Grange and the thousand acres of land that went with it.

At first, Robson had been interested in the relationship between the new owner and the quiet beautiful girl—for that is how he thought of her—whom he had brought with him. But as autumn gave way to winter and not by a single word or deed could he detect anything but the most correct—even cold—behaviour displayed towards each other, he had become disappointed and then slightly bored. Although his life was certainly easier—for Mr Frayne and Miss Delafield spent most of each week in London—nevertheless, the Beresfords had been much more colourful employers. With them, there had always been something going on. True, towards the end of their time at Wilcot—which had finally been terminated by the improvidence of an elder son—the old Dowager herself had been a bit of a trial, especially after she had started taking against her grandson, Master Paul, and locking him up in the tower suite which Miss Delafield now occupied. Robson could recall one occasion when he had had to send the chauffeur to bring the child's father back from the hunting-field because the old woman had thrown away the key. Nowadays, such traumas were a thing of the past. Robson could not imagine the present inhabitants ever raising their voices or doing anything untoward except, of course, going in for this business of living together, unmarried, under the same roof, which he knew was causing endless speculation amongst those who did not have such a good opportunity for witnessing, as he did, that whatever other things Mr Frayne and Miss Delafield might have in common, sex would not appear to be one of them.

"I tell you," he said to his wife one Monday evening when they were alone in the small stable flat which they occupied at the back of the house, "there's nothing in it. She just drives him about and acts as his secretary. It's my belief he looks on her as a daughter. Just think of the age gap. He must be at least twenty-five years older."

"Daughter, my foot," snorted Mrs Robson. "He's a *man*, isn't he?" She reckoned she knew all about men. After all, she had had trouble with Robson over a chit of a young parlourmaid not all that many years ago, although she supposed her husband would have conveniently forgotten this.

"But Miss Delafield's a *lady*, Elsie. Sticks out a mile. You said yourself she keeps a photograph of a parson on her dressing-table."

"That doesn't necessarily follow," replied Mrs Robson, although she was not sure that such a statement carried much weight. She only knew that, the weekend before last, when Ellen, the housemaid who usually took up Miss Delafield's early morning tea, had gone down with 'flu and she had been obliged to undertake the task herself because the other girls on the staff appeared about to succumb likewise, she had found, at the bottom of the stairs leading to the tower, a man's monogrammed silk handkerchief. She had picked it up, put it with the other washing waiting to be done on Monday morning and said nothing to anyone, not even her husband. She knew her job. She was an experienced, formidable, first-class housekeeper of a large establishment. It was one thing to give Robson her opinion of their employer in private, but quite another to give any hint of tangible incriminating evidence against either him or Miss Delafield, for whom she actually felt sorry. There was enough tittle-tattle going on already, not only amongst the Wilcot staff but also in the village. Besides, the handkerchief had not been actually *on* the tower steps. It was on the landing. Mr Frayne could have dropped it on his way to. . . But, here again, Mrs Robson was at a loss to know where her employer could possibly have been going unless it was to the back stairs, an area where neither he nor, for that matter, any male Beresford—except Master Paul—had ever been known to wander.

Harvey Frayne had, indeed, visited the tower suite on the occasion in question, something he had only done once since he had first looked over the Grange, when he had simply gone up to check that the decoration and furnishing had been attended to according to his instructions. Now, however, he had spent an hour and a half there between twelve and one thirty a.m. and was well satisfied with what had taken place. He found that his instinct had not let him down. Rather in the same way as he conducted his increasingly prosperous business dealings in London, seeking out the most likely-looking property in which to invest for good returns, he had been aware, ever since he had clapped eyes on Rose Delafield at a party in Chelsea the previous summer, that she was the sort of girl who would, given a little time and tuition, turn into exactly the kind of companion he required: well-bred, good-looking, amenable, outwardly shy and retiring and therefore deceptively respectable, but who would, once her natural defences had been broken down, become a willing and even a passionate lover.

He had been prepared to wait quite a while before making any approaches in this last connection. He had been surprised that the psychological moment had presented itself so much sooner than expected. But one Sunday afternoon that autumn, something had occurred which made him feel that he would not be rebuffed should he decide to climb the round stone staircase to the tower after Rose had retired for the night. They had been walking through Folly Woods, the trees still ablaze with red and yellow and golden leaves, and he had managed to save her from falling when she had caught the hem of her skirt while climbing a stile. He noticed that after he had finally helped her to jump down, she had not immediately broken away but had remained, eyelids lowered, her half-parted lips rather too near to his own. He had let go of her abruptly, almost roughly, and walked on ahead. Although they had seemed quite alone in the woods, he knew well enough there were eyes and ears everywhere in the countryside. He was never going to be such a fool as manifestly to make public that which, however much speculation there might always be, he intended to keep absolutely private. He had been annoyed to find that his feelings had not been under better control in Folly Woods and had set off for home at such a furious rate that Rose had scarcely been able to keep up with him.

One thing about which Harvey Frayne was quite sure was that he would never marry again. He had made this abundantly clear to Rose at the outset of their association. He did not want her to get ideas. Neither did he want her, at that stage, to think of him as anything other than an employer. At the very first interview he had explained that he was separated from his wife, who lived abroad with their only daughter. Mrs Thora Frayne was a Catholic and there was no question of a divorce. (He naturally did not add that even if there were, he had no intention of entering the same trap twice.) He simply informed Rose that he was looking for an amanuensis—a word she subsequently had to look up in the dictionary—who would type his letters, drive his car—mostly on long journeys only—and who was used to country life, as he had just acquired an estate in the west country.

He went on to say that if he had understood her aright, she appeared to possess all three qualifications. He would appreciate it if she would arrange the flowers and act as hostess in both his homes, but the latter task would not be onerous as he entertained little. He mentioned that he was thinking of taking up shooting later on, which might necessitate giving a few shooting parties but this was something still very much in the air. As for the general running of his two establishments, he employed a married couple both in London and the country, together with other adequate staff. He would be willing to pay Rose two hundred and fifty pounds per annum and her keep. He hoped she would find his offer acceptable. For so secretive a man he had been quite communicative.

He recalled how she had stared at him, wide-eyed yet composed, her thick auburn hair parted in the middle and swept demurely back into a bun at the nape of her neck. Her face was oval, her complexion creamy and flawless. He felt there to be a distinct Mona Lisa-like quality about her except that her mouth was fuller, giving more than a hint of hidden sexuality. She had sat very still, something he greatly admired in women. With her high-collared white blouse and plain navy suit, she might have been a governess applying for the post of looking after the child he had scarcely seen. He was unsure whether she was oblivious to or merely acquiescent of the somewhat unconventional proposition he had put before her.

"I shall, of course," she had replied, at length, "have to ask Aunt Jackson."

"Aunt Jackson?"

"Yes. My father's widowed sister. The lady you met at the party in Chelsea who has been caring for me since he died. She's an artist. I've been staying at her studio flat while doing my secretarial training."

"I see. Well, perhaps you would let me know if you can

accept the post as soon as possible."

He had risen, dismissively, and held out his hand. Her own was cold to the touch, another point he had noted in her favour. Though young and inexperienced, she had remained completely unflustered throughout the entire interview. He had stood at the window of his Mayfair house watching her slim figure disappear in the direction of Park Lane. He believed she would come to him. He had a clear recollection of Aunt Jackson, a large Bohemian-looking lady with a long cigarette holder. He had a feeling that concern over the propriety of her ward's prospective move would come secondary to wanting the girl out of her way.

Harvey Frayne had not been wrong. Belle Jackson had called to see him the following day. She was by no means the kind of woman whom he would have thought of as the sister of a clergyman. She had smoked a couple of Turkish cigarettes, drunk three glasses of sherry, informed him that Rose was sweet, if not too bright, that she herself was hoping to make a protracted visit to Egypt in the very near future, in order to make sketches of the pyramids, and she would be delighted to feel that the girl would not be left alone in London. Without putting it in so many words, she managed to convey the impression that, as she considered Harvey to be a complete gentleman, she had no hesitation in entrusting her ward to his care. She could only hope, she had said—somewhat naïvely, he felt, on departing—that Rose would give satisfaction.

Five months later, as Harvey Frayne had descended the tower steps at Wilcot Grange, he had smiled to himself to think that Aunt Jackson's hopes had been more than fulfilled. The following morning he had been annoyed to find that he had mislaid one of his handkerchiefs. He was not in the habit of making mistakes. On the way back to London he had even gone as far as to ask Rose whether she had come across it, despite the fact that he did not want to refer in any way to what had happened between them in the hours of darkness. It was best for that to remain something scarcely acknowledged, secreted, above all others, in the many water-tight compartments which went to make up his complicated, repressed and sadly unsatisfactory life.

When he noticed his chauffeuse flush, he found his anger rising. The last thing he wanted was for Rose to become emotional. He did not believe in sentiment. He did not require love. He wanted a certain kind of companionship and he needed sex. He was relieved, even if disappointed, when he heard her reply, levelly, as she slowed down the Rolls on the outskirts of Winchester, "No, I'm afraid I haven't seen it."

2

With the approach of Christmas, Mrs Robson found she had many more things on her mind than her employer's relationship with his secretary. She had no idea of his plans for the festive season. Was he to be in residence? Might not Miss Delafield want to visit the clergyman whose photograph had, according to Ellen, mysteriously disappeared from her dressing-table? Would there be other company in the house? How many puddings should she make? Usually, by this time, they were all finished, securely tied down in basins, lining the pantry shelves. Surely Mr Frayne and Miss Delafield weren't going to spend the holiday at the Grange all by themselves in complete isolation? And what about the party for the village children which the Beresfords had always given in the house for as long as Mrs Robson could remember? Such matters would have to be resolved and the sooner the better. If Mr Frayne was not going to broach the subject then she, Mrs Robson, would have to do so herself. It was impossible to glean anything from her husband, who seemed more interested these days in putting his feet up and poring over the competitions in *John Bull*.

Mrs Robson knew that it was possible just to drop a word in Miss Delafield's ear, but somehow she did not want to do that. She had never gone in for what she felt to be roundabout ways. Mr Frayne was her employer. Miss Delafield most certainly was not.

Towards the end of November, Mrs Robson decided to accost Harvey Frayne after breakfast one morning as he was making for his study.

"Please sir, could I have a word with you?"

He looked at first surprised and then irritated. He had already had a telephone call from the rector asking if he might come to see him later that day, a day which Harvey had set aside for the express purpose of going over the estate with his manager and making some definite plans for the future, which would include the reversion of the shooting rights which had temporarily been leased to James Buckley, a neighbouring tenant farmer. However, Harvey felt that he could not very well refuse to see his housekeeper, although as he ushered her into his study he made it quite plain that he had little time to spare.

"It's about Christmas, sir," she said, coming straight to the point as she stood in front of his desk, a sturdy well-corseted figure who looked at her employer out of very direct blue eyes. He did not think he liked her. It occurred to him that she might well have found his handkerchief.

"Christmas, Mrs Robson?" He affected an air of puzzled impatience.

"Yes. It's little more than four weeks away, sir. I was wondering . . . how many there might be to cater for."

"Ah, I see. Yes, of course. I suppose I haven't given the matter much thought. Perhaps one or two friends from London. I must let you know. I'm afraid. . ." and here he relaxed a little and gave a small deprecatory smile, "I've never been an exactly Christmassy sort of person, Mrs Robson."

"I see. Thank you, sir." His unexpected description of himself had intrigued her. With his clipped speech, tall spare figure, hooded eyes and slightly hooked nose, the memory of a book she had read in her youth came suddenly flooding back to Mrs Robson, although she knew that Mr Frayne was not exactly a Scrooge. He might expect good service but he paid well for it. With her sharp mother-wit, she sensed, rather than fully comprehended, that her employer was the kind of man who would give, materially, because he could not give in any other way.

Harvey had sat down while they had been speaking, but now he rose in order to effect his housekeeper's departure. But Mrs Robson stood her ground.

"There is just one other thing, sir."

"Yes?" His impatience bordered on rudeness.

"In the past there has always been a party at the Grange for the children of the village. All between the ages of three and ten. Usually the day before Christmas Eve."

"Really?" So *that* was probaby what the rector wanted to see him about. "I will think about it, Mrs Robson," he continued, making it plain that the interview was finally at an end.

After his housekeeper had gone, Harvey stood frowning for a few minutes. He was glad to be forewarned. Obviously, a party at the Grange was quite out of the question, unthinkable in fact. A whole lot of snotty-nosed kids running amok through his precious possessions, possibly throwing jelly at his latest Laura Knight. He would write a cheque. A handsome one. They could have their party at the village hall. The local inhabitants would have to understand that things had changed. What had happened in the Beresfords' time did not automatically have to happen now. Besides, he was, to all outward appearances, unmarried. It would be most unsuitable. However much he might not have wanted to acknowlege the fact to himself, Rose was now his mistress. Parties for little children needed to be conducted under the auspices of a wife, even though he was well aware that the present lady of Wilcot, had she but had marriage lines, would have filled the role admirably.

Rose was more than aware of this herself. She knew exactly why the Reverend Mr Courtenay was coming to see Harvey that day. Such things had an infallible way of percolating back to her. Some weeks ago, she had heard all about the annual Christmas party at the Grange through one of the under-gardener's children. "Miss," little Roger had said, "which day will the party be?" It had made her think of all the ones that had taken place at the Manor in the village of Netherbury, where she had been brought up. She could see, as if it were yesterday, the owner, the Dowager Lady Prestcott, and her father, with his head and shoulders festooned with streamers and she herself helping him because, sadly, her mother had died of pneumonia when Rose had been only five.

At a very young age she had become accustomed to responsibility. As the years went by she did her best to take her mother's place. She realised that she was the only daughter of the parson, from whom service was expected. Soon, it became second nature to care, not only for her father but also for his flock. When she was seventeen and Henry Delafield had succumbed to the same fatal illness which had carried off his wife, fighting for his last breath in the large, damp, chilling rectory on the Norfolk Broads, Rose had, for a time, been inconsolable. Swept up by Aunt Jackson into a strange uncongenial milieu, she had gone about her secretarial training in a state of numb resignation. But her father had left exactly four hundred and fifty pounds and she knew that she had to earn her own living. It had scarcely been surprising that, when Harvey Frayne had made the offer of her present post, she had welcomed the idea of looking after an older man again. It was a role she understood, even needed. That it had come to include sex was something which confused and bothered her, particularly her own surprising response to it, but she did her best not to let Harvey know this. She recognised that the two men of whom she had any experience, though of widely different characters, nevertheless had certain traits in common: they valued, both in themselves and others, calmness, efficiency and the ability to cope with personal problems. "As a parson," her father had once said to her, with a wry smile, "I am not really meant to have any troubles of my own. Others come to me with theirs." And then, rather surprisingly and pathetically, he had added, "But I am, after all, a human being. Remember St Matthew, my dear? 'The spirit is indeed willing, but the flesh is weak'."

Rose had been fifteen then, the first stirrings of sexuality within her. She had pondered for some time over her father's remark. It had never occurred to her before to think of him as a man who had been married and who had—and here another biblical phrase had come into her mind—begotten her. She had pushed the thought quickly away. It had seemed repugnant, even though she was singularly uninformed about the facts of life. When, some time later, Aunt Jackson had thrust a book called *The Cradle Ship* into her hands, remarking, cryptically, that it would help her over things it was time she knew, Rose had pounced on it avidly, only to become increasingly disappointed. Such information as there had been was couched in such a vague sentimental way that Rose had learned little, if anything from reading it. The following January, Henry Delafield had died. Since then, until

Harvey Frayne's midnight sortie to the tower suite, she had tried to pretend that, so far as she was concerned, sex was as closed a book as *The Cradle Ship*.

But now all that was altered. Possibly because she had for so long, and with such resolve, denied her own natural instincts, she found herself overwhelmed by them. She was not only powerless to refuse her employer's advances, she actively welcomed them. She retired early at the weekends although, by tacit understanding, Harvey never appeared before twelve when, presumably, he reckoned that no servants would be about. Even then, he took the greatest care. His nocturnal visits were clandestine in the extreme, his route illuminated, if necessary, by torchlight, his lovemaking conducted either in total darkness or, sometimes, with the aid of the moon shining through uncurtained windows. He spoke hardly at all. The very strangeness and secrecy which surrounded these occasions seemed to Rose to give them an added thrill. After he had gone she would lie awake, missing him, wishing that she need not spend the rest of the night alone. She would then, somewhat ambiguously, start wanting their relationship to be regularised by marriage, while at the same time knowing, deep down, that the element of risk, even guilt, was somehow necessary for them both.

After a while, she would drift into an uneasy sleep, awakening the next morning wondering just how she had come to find herself in such unusual circumstances, the pleasurable memory of the previous night evaporating as she noted—or thought she noted—the sly glance of Ellen as she brought her early morning tea or, later on, the look of disrespect, as she felt, on the face of Mrs Robson. She would become prim Miss Delafield again, completely self-effacing, going about her duties more reserved and conscientiously than ever. When visitors, such as the rector or, perhaps, a neighbour like James Buckley, were known to be calling, she made it her business to be well out of the way, back in the tower suite, typing, reading, sewing or listening to her portable wireless set.

It was, therefore, an acute embarrassment when she found herself actually crossing the hall as the Reverend Mr

Courtenay, a quarter of an hour early, was being shown in on the same day as Mrs Robson had tackled Harvey about Christmas. Almost, Rose felt, she had been caught in a compromising act, that she had no business to be where she was, that if only she could hurry through the baize door she could dissociate herself from both the rector and her surroundings. Mr Courtenay was, alas, too quick for her.

"My dear Miss Delafield!"

He came striding towards her, large, red-faced, full of bonhomie, the antithesis of the saintly-looking pale-faced character who had been her father. She felt that Mr Courtenay accepted her, that not for one moment did he envisage her as anything other than what she was purported to be: Harvey Frayne's secretary who, owing to unavoidable circumstances, was fulfilling a vital if somewhat unique position in the Wilcot ménage.

"Good-evening, Rector," she said, holding out her hand.

He shook it warmly, affable in the extreme. He did not appear to bear her any ill-will for no longer coming to Evensong, something which, like the putting away of her father's photograph, she could no longer face since Harvey's nocturnal sojourns to the tower suite. Presumably, Mr Courtenay could not possibly have guessed what sort of woman she really was. He was too innocent, too unworldly. Or was he? Could it be, perhaps, that he was giving her the benefit of the doubt because—and here she chided herself for her own worldly thoughts—he was more concerned in keeping in with the lord of the manor? After all, Harvey Frayne was the man who held so many purse strings, to whom, theoretically, the Reverend Mr Courtenay owed his living.

He seemed surprised, even disappointed when, after a few more pleasantries, she asked to be excused on the grounds that she still had some typing to do. It was actually a true enough statment. Harvey had asked her if she would type out some hand-written notes he had made of all that had taken place between his manager and himself earlier that day.

She began moving towards the baize door while Robson, who had been hovering in the background during their conversation, made another move to conduct Mr Courtenay in the opposite direction towards Harvey's study. As she said goodbye, she realised how much their brief encounter had saddened her. It was so obvious that the rector had been hoping for feminine support at his meeting with the owner of Wilcot, perhaps an assurance from her that she would supervise the children's party.

She knew that the possibility of this was as remote as Harvey agreeing to the event taking place at the Grange. She could almost see him writing out a cheque, hear his decisive, faintly gravelly voice saying, as he picked up his pen, "Would ten pounds cover it, Rector?" and the reply, "Oh, my dear Mr Frayne, that is more than adequate. Most generous."

The matter would be closed. Harvey would have bought his peace and privacy in the same way as, sadly, she had come to realise he had bought her. He had already doubled her salary, explaining, in an almost monosyllabic fashion, that it would be better than buying her jewellery which might be noticed by the staff.

3

On December 23rd, Rose drove the ten miles to Fordingham station to collect Carl Scholte, a portrait painter, and his wife, Elena, who were to spend Christmas at Wilcot Grange. She had met them but once, in London, and recalled a strangely ill-assorted couple: the man, short, fat and ugly with a marked guttural accent, the woman tall, fair and thin, with a distinct Nordic look about her.

Rose felt nervous as she waited in the station car-park, wishing that Harvey had acompanied her. For one thing, she wondered if the Scholtes would recognise her, as their previous meeting had been of the briefest kind. She had simply been introduced to them at a Private View of Carl's work to which, somewhat surprisingly, Harvey had asked if she would like to accompany him. Since then, however, she had begun noticing that whereas at Wilcot he continued to keep her at a distance—other than at night—in London he seemed increasingly forthcoming, even though, here, they were never lovers. She was aware, of course, that his Mayfair home did not lend itself to secret nocturnal visits in the same way as his country one. It was a tall house, in which there were several floors but only one staircase, and her own room and bathroom happened to be situated just beneath the attics where Harvey's married couple slept. Sometimes, Rose felt that the extraordinary difference between the life she was expected to lead in London compared to that in the country was as confusing and hard to accept as the discovery of her unexpected response to her employer's sexual advances.

She wondered what Mr and Mrs Scholte would think of her, whether they would both sit in the back of the Rolls, treating her as none other than what she purported to be: a chauffeuse-cum secretary to whom they would not think it necessary to show more than formal politeness. Did they understand that she was, in effect, to be their hostess over the

19

holiday, that in order to boost her sadly lacking confidence she had visited a Bond Street couturier and bought a fashionable—even daring—black velvet evening dress, thanks to her sudden rise in salary? On the other hand, as the Scholtes came from the artistic world, it was possible they had already taken it for granted she was Harvey's mistress. Rose hardly knew which attitude she would prefer them to adopt. She only knew that at least Harvey seemed happy to have got hold of these particular last-minute guests, partly, she suspected, because they came from the unconventional milieu in which he felt himself more accepted and partly because of his increasing interest in modern painting. How much the latter was from an aesthetic, possessive or investment point of view, Rose was still unsure.

When the bell rang announcing the arrival of the London train, she got out of the car, bought herself a platform ticket and went to stand just inside the barrier. Her father had always stressed how necessary it was to be actually *on* the platform when awaiting guests. "Otherwise," he would say, "it looks as if you aren't prepared to pay for the privilege of giving them a proper greeting".

As the crowd of alighting passengers thinned, she caught sight of Carl and Elena half way along the platform, arguing. On hurrying towards them it appeared that Elena wanted to engage a porter and her husband was objecting on the grounds that he could perfectly well carry their incredible amount of luggage, which included an easel and some canvasses inadequately tied up with string.

Elena almost fell on Rose with cries of relief. Feeling equally grateful, Rose realised that she had been worrying unnecessarily about her dubious status. Even the truculent Carl ceased protesting as she appeared; a hovering porter was engaged and soon the Scholtes, along with all their accoutrements, were safely ensconced in the Rolls, Elena electing to sit in the front with Rose.

"So lovely," she kept saying, on the journey back to Wilcot. "Such beautiful country." Often, she would turn her head and repeat these remarks to her husband. At one point, where the road descended from a high ridge of downs, she exclaimed,

"Just look at that view, Carl. Would you not like to paint it?" to which his answer came as a complete surprise to Rose, "You forget, Elena. I am commissioned. Harvey is my next subject."

As they drove through the village of Wilcot itself there was quite a little crowd of mothers with their offspring converging on the village hall and Rose explained that it was the day of the children's party. Such information was obviously of but slight interest to Elena and none whatsoever to her husband. It was plain to Rose that their guests were not parents and had about as much connection with the English countryside as their host. With a feeling of sadness, she drove on, swept through the gates of the Grange and swung the car round into the forecourt, drawing up at the front door just as Robson, with his infallible sense of timing and ceremony born of long practice, opened it to receive them.

Throughout the rest of the day, it seemed to Rose that it was easier to relate to the Scholtes—particularly Elena—when she was alone with them. Although Harvey had come into the hall behind Robson and welcomed them most courteously, his efforts at conversation, especially during dinner when Robson was present, were somehow forced. Rose could not imagine how they were all four going to get through the next few days, apart from the sittings which would be taking place in connection with Carl's portrait of Harvey. Indoor games, such as bridge, seemed out of the question as no one knew how to play any, except Elena who said she was never averse to a game of racing demon. No entertainment of a more positive kind had been planned, other than a trip to Fordingham for last-minute shopping on Christmas Eve, a visit from the town's carol singers later that evening, church on Christmas Day—to which Rose was determined to go, even if no one accompanied her—and a drive to the Meet of the local hounds at Picket's End on Boxing Day. The only really formal event was a dinner to be given that night for James Buckley and his wife—all in all, hardly an inspiring agenda.

It was Harvey who had suggested inviting the Buckleys to Wilcot on hearing that the Scholtes would be coming. Had he but known it, this had caused much soul-searching in the

Buckley household. James's wife, Anne, had at first refused, point-blank, to countenance the idea of setting foot inside the Wilcot ménage and had done her best to insist that the invitation be declined. As far as she was concerned, it would be tantamount to condoning an illicit relationship. In keeping with the rest of the local community, she found Harvey Frayne *persona non grata*. "Don't forget, James," she had said, "we have a daughter. Susan is coming up fifteen. Not all that much younger than Miss Delafield. If we go to Wilcot, what sort of example shall be setting? We shall be parents who openly advocate free love." To which, James Buckley had replied, levelly, "But we don't *know*, my dear, that anything of that sort is going on. Surely Mr Frayne must be given the benefit of the doubt. He has been most straightforward and generous about the shooting, even offering to wait a further season before having the rights revert to him, rather than cause me any difficulty or disappointment. He obviously wishes to be friendly."

"Of course he does," Anne Buckley had snapped. "He'd do anything to be accepted socially round here. But he must realise he can't bring a chit of a girl down from London, live with her under the same roof and get away with it. No one else in the neighbourhood goes to Wilcot Grange."

"Well, if they don't," her husband had then answered, "I can't see how the poor man's going to get a shooting party together next winter. I think you'll find that people will come around to the situation in time. Look, Anne, give it a try. If you don't like it, you needn't go again. I can't see that dinner on Boxing night is going to harm us, or Susan."

Grudgingly, Anne Buckley had at last agreed. She loved her husband and, as far as possible, relied on his judgment. She knew what shooting meant to him and that whatever happened she would never have the heart to try to stop him going, as a guest, to Harvey Frayne's own parties in a year's time.

It therefore came about that on Boxing night the Buckleys were expected at Wilcot at seven forty-five for eight p.m. Rose came downstairs well beforehand, wearing her new dress which she had decided to keep for the occasion. She was alone in the drawing-room, standing by the huge open fireplace, one arm on the back of a high wing chair, as Carl Scholte came in to join her. She was at once aware of his undisguised admiration. Half way across the room, he stopped, held up a hand and said, "Don't move." Then he advanced slowly, regarding her from this angle and that until, finally, he said, "No, the first pose was the best."

"But I wasn't posing." She found herself speaking to him quite naturally, albeit blushing and laughing. "Harvey is your subject," she went on.

"But you are my next," he replied, walking over to a side table and helping himself to a whisky. "And in that frock, please. I hadn't realised until now. Silly of me. . . ."

Before she could answer, Harvey himself was in the room and she knew that he, too, seemed to be regarding her in a new light, that because of the black dress she was wearing which showed off her figure to perfection, something had happened, that she had suddenly acquired a new poise, a self-assurance that she had never thought it possible to possess. What was more, she knew, after the little party was assembled, that she was a woman with power, that she alone was the one to whom all three men in the room were drawn. Neither Anne Buckley, in her unobtrusive green taffeta, nor Elena, with her fantastic diamond necklace, could command the same attention.

Long after she was in bed that night, the feeling of euphoria remained. She remembered how she had been able to converse, to initiate a conversation, to talk to James Buckley as an equal, especially concerning country matters, about which her knowledge had obviously surprised and impressed him. "My father," she had explained, "was the rector of a large parish on the Norfolk Broads." She had smiled as she said it, inadvertently leaning forward a little so that the neckline of her dress revealed just a fraction more of the top of her firm small breasts. The wine had made her happy, relaxed. She had ceased to feel guilty that the Reverend Henry Delafield's only daughter was now a mistress.

When Harvey Frayne silently opened her door in the early hours of the morning, she still felt the same sense of freedom and abandonment. As he slipped into bed beside her, it seemed there was a lot to be said for her new way of life, especially when she heard his whispered words, "You looked so beautiful tonight. I'm afraid I couldn't keep away."

4

"You're looking very well, my dear."

Aunt Jackson was giving Rose lunch at the Coq D'Or. They had hardly seen each other since the previous summer, for Belle Jackson's wanderlust had taken her not only to Egypt but to several continental countries as well, including Germany. "What is happening there is most impressive," she said. "This man Hitler seems to be a great leader. He's restoring national pride. Would you like curry, Rose? They do it awfully well here."

"If it's all the same to you, Aunt J, perhaps I could have the *sole meunière?*"

A year ago, Rose knew that she would never have dared not to fall in with whatever her aunt had suggested. The latter, too, made a mental note of the same fact. There was no doubt that the difference in her niece was quite astonishing. This was no longer the shy, countrified, eager-to-please girl with a rather severe hair-style and sensible clothes. Rose looked positively soignée. She was wearing a figure-hugging fawn suit trimmed with astrakhan and a little astrakhan pill-box hat to match, from which auburn curls appeared to frame a carefully made-up face. As she peeled off a pair of fawn suede gloves, she revealed expertly manicured finger-nails.

It was obvious to Belle Jackson that her former ward had had what people referred to nowadays as "experience", and she was well aware that the eyes of several men in the restaurant kept straying in the direction of their table. Belle wondered what her brother would think of the situation. As his sister, she supposed she had failed him in allowing his only daughter to take a step which, had she really stopped to think about and not been so keen on going abroad, she might have known would turn out in the way it had. Although never, in her wildest dreams, would she have envisaged the speed with which a rather gentle flower had been transformed into a

25

gorgeous, even exotic, bloom. Belle tried not to feel guilty. The damage had been done. And Rose did look extraordinarily happy.

"I simply must let you know something, Aunt J," she chattered away gaily, as the waiter brought their order, "my portrait is to be hung in this year's summer exhibition at the R.A."

Nothing could have given Belle Jackson better proof—had she needed it—of her niece's new status. Girls such as Rose did not have their portraits painted unless they were something very much more than an ordinary secretary.

"May I ask who the artist is?" Belle enquired.

"Someone whom everybody calls an up-and-coming man. Carl Scholte. You've probably heard of him."

"Indeed I have. There was a portrait by him hung in the Academy last year. *Elena* I think it was called."

"That's his wife."

"Really? You know them both?"

"Yes. They're friends of Harvey. They spent last Christmas at Wilcot."

"I see."

Belle saw a lot of things, now. This beautiful young thing in front of her had entered another world, a world that she herself understood and in which she, too, had a small part. She might not have arrived there so quickly or by the same route as her niece. She had certainly been a virgin when she married Gordon Jackson, but nevertheless she had run away from a doctor's strictly orthodox home—where she had been attending a local art school—in order to do so, causing untold anxiety to her parents and barely concealed admiration on the part of Henry, her younger brother. In time, the rift in family relationships had been healed. Gordon Jackson, a tea-planter, had prospered. They had returned from India at various intervals and stayed in the Delafield household. Here, Belle had shown her parents some of the striking and original paintings she had done of Muslim and Hindu women in their native setting. George Delafield and his wife had been duly impressed, although Belle knew they would have preferred it if she had produced grandchildren.

Then, when only thirty-seven, Gordon Jackson had been killed while driving with his manager in a truck which had swerved into a ravine during the monsoon. Belle had returned to England, by no means impecunious, but with a determination—despite her grief—to augment her fortunes by her own artistic talents. She had not done at all badly. She might not be in the same class as Carl Scholte but she had a definite, if limited, following, mostly amongst retired army officers or civil servants who appreciated her ability to capture on canvas the scenes they remembered of their active working days. Her pictures sold well enough to bring her in sufficient money to satisfy her desire for continued travel, so that she spent roughly half the year in London and half abroad. By the time she was forty she had become her own person, emancipated, freed from the doubts, restrictions and inhibitions which she suspected had ruined her brother's life. For although Henry had gone into the church, she knew he had held other aspirations, possibly of being an actor, and that, deep down, he shared with her a certain wildness, a desire to flout convention, tendencies which it was all too obvious were now coming out in Rose. Belle wondered just how long it had taken before her niece had been seduced, what precautions were being taken to prevent her becoming pregnant, although she did not think she need worry too much on that score. A man like Harvey Frayne would have known what he was about, probably sending Rose off to some first-class gynaecologist to get herself, as it was termed, "fixed up". She studied, once again, the animated face before her, for the moment with the eyelids lowered, Rose having just caught the glance of a man two tables away. There will be trouble, Belle said to herself, albeit fascinated by the metamorphosis.

"You always go to the Private View at the R.A. each summer, don't you, Aunt J?" Those eyes were now looking straight at Belle. "Perhaps we could all join up. Harvey. The Scholtes. Have lunch together somewhere."

"Yes, dear. That would be very nice."

And presumably, Belle thought, Harvey would be paying. Rose could make him pay. She had youth, looks and a tantalising mixture of vulnerability and awareness. It must be irresistible to an ageing man. But where would it lead? How could it last?

Belle Jackson parted from her niece that day with a strange unease. Yet, as she saw the slim figure disappear into a taxi, she knew that Rose had at least experienced something which, despite her own not altogether unexciting life, she had never known. Except for a pair of rather fine brown eyes, Belle knew she was a plain woman. Gordon Jackson had been her one and only love. As she took the underground back to her flat, she wondered what it must be like, at so young an age, to have the power to ensnare a man like Harvey Frayne who she had heard, through the grapevine, was well on the way to becoming a millionaire.

Rose headed straight for Bond Street and spent the rest of the afternoon shopping. She was hunting for some gold kid shoes to wear with the cream satin dress and gold lamé coatee which she proposed to don for the first time that evening. Harvey was taking her to a party given by an art critic called Stephen Forman who lived near Holland Park and she was determined to make an impression. She understood that, although young, their host was influential and his favourable opinion of *Portrait of Rose* might make all the difference to its success when it was shown at the Academy in a month's time.

As she came down into the drawing-room prior to setting out, she was delighted to notice that her new *ensemble* had, at any rate, certainly met with Harvey's approval. The look in his eyes emboldened her to do something she had never done before. She went across and gave him a light kiss on his cheek.

She was both astonished and angry at the way he instantly recoiled.

"Please, Rose. Not . . . here."

"Oh, for goodness sake. Why not?" She tossed the loose curls, her rejected lips now forming a definite pout.

"Corbett might come in. He's gone to hail a taxi. I've told you, I want no demonstration of affection in public. Come along. We should be on our way." On these occasions, he never asked her to drive.

Throughout the journey she remained silent, studiously looking out of the window, absently noting the islands of

yellow daffodils in Hyde Park as the breeze blew them hither
and thither in the fading light of the spring evening.

Harvey Frayne knew that he had hurt her and was suddenly
afraid. After he had paid off the taxi and they were walking
towards the steps of their destination, he said quickly, "I'm
sorry, Rose." She flashed him a brilliant smile of forgiveness
and when, a few moments later, they entered a room in which
there was a far larger gathering than either had anticipated,
she seemed to do so in triumph. She noted, with satisfaction,
not only the charming and deferential way in which her
debonair host greeted her but, just as it had happened earlier
that day, the eyes of most of the men in the room now turned
in her direction.

It was only a few days later when Harvey said, almost
casually, "I've decided to sell this house. I've bought another
one in Belgravia. Would you like to see it?"

Wonderingly, she accompanied him there. It was empty but
he appeared to have the key. It was a far larger establishment
than his present one, and possessed two entirely separate
single suites on the second floor.

"I thought perhaps you might like this one," he remarked,
walking over to the window. "It's the quietest and looks out
on to the gardens at the back."

She could see at once why he had made the purchase. Their
lovemaking would no longer be confined to the country. It
occurred to her that her conduct earlier that week had
precipitated matters. The feeling of power she had over him
was stronger than ever.

"While the move takes place," he said, later that evening, "I
thought we might go abroad. There are certain structural
improvements needed in Belgravia, especially to the kitchen
quarters. How would you feel about staying in Monte Carlo
before it gets too hot?"

"*Monte Carlo?*"

He smiled slightly at her obvious pleasure. "Yes, I've been
thinking, too, that rather than asking you to drive, we might
take the Blue Train. It would be more of a holiday for you."

"*The Blue Train?*" She repeated his words again. Her eyes
widened, her lips parted in the way he had come to know so

well. He could sense her rising excitement. The very words had conjured up for her photographs she had seen, reports she had read in newspapers and magazines. Her mind flew to her wardrobe. She would need some lightweight travelling wear, outfits for the beach, some of those new baggy colourful beach pyjamas which were all the rage. She wanted to do more than merely go across the room and give him a peck on the cheek. She wanted to throw her arms around him. But, wisely, she desisted.

As they parted and said goodnight, almost formally, she went upstairs thinking, as she so often did, about the strange character of the man with whom she seemed to have thrown in her lot. By taking her abroad on the Blue Train, surely he was virtually flaunting their relationship. Yet, for the time being, he still appeared to want to keep her at arm's length, other than on certain strictly private occasions.

5

Harvey bought Carl Scholte's *Portrait of Rose* for one hundred pounds and immediately presented it to her. It had been acclaimed the artist's best to date, particularly by Stephen Forman. In a leading national newspaper he had described Carl as having "captured the essence of his subject: a young woman not yet fully aware of her strange allure". Others had used words such as "enchanting" or "appealing", one going as far as to refer to an "innocent Lorelei".

"You might like to hang it in your new sitting-room when we move to Belgravia," Harvey had said.

In many ways, Rose would have preferred her portrait to have been hung downstairs, in the hall or the drawing-room, where more people might see it. But she realised that Harvey would never agree to that. It would be such an admission of the way things were between them. Yet, after the picture's publicity, she felt that everyone, including all the servants in both homes, must now be well aware of their relationship.

In London, it hardly seemed to matter. At Wilcot, however, she knew that she was still far from being accepted socially, other than by a few people such as James Buckley and the owners of neighbouring farms or estates who had their eye on a day's shooting. It was all too obvious that it was always the men who were apt to be agreeable. Hardly any woman, not even Anne Buckley, was more than formally polite to her. When she felt snubbed, as she had been by Lady Matheson, the organiser of the annual flower show, she found herself bursting with resentment, not only towards Elsa Matheson but Harvey himself. Why couldn't he get a divorce? Was his wife *really* a Catholic? Even if she were, surely he could do something about it? Divorce, in such circumstances, was sometimes obtainable, wasn't it?

Often, it was all she could do not to broach the subject to him, but each time something warned her against it. Harvey was such a curious man: unpredictable, contradictory, even self-deluding. Did he really suppose that just because they behaved so correctly towards each other in public no one else had any idea about what went on in the tower suite? Or that when they had gone to Monte Carlo they had lived like brother and sister, despite Harvey's insistence on separate apartments at the hotel? It was almost as if he was able to treat their lovemaking as something which happened to two other people. Certainly, both of them then seemed to turn into two very different creatures. In this respect they were ideally suited. He had known instinctively how to please her. She had learnt quickly how to please him. She was looking forward to such occasions happening more frequently when they moved house in London, while at the same time becoming increasingly anxious that the situation should be regularised.

As the summer gave way to autumn, her frustration in this respect was not helped by the growing rumours concerning the King and Mrs Simpson. Rose had at first become aware of these while she and Harvey had been abroad, where the foreign press was reporting on the couple's holiday in the Adriatic on board the yacht *Nahlin*. Back in England, when the British newspapers could no longer maintain their conspiracy of silence, she avidly read every available detail about Edward VIII's apparent obsession with this American divorcee. Would he or would he not throw up his throne in order to marry her? If only Harvey, Rose thought, would behave more like the King, make no bones about his feelings, do everything he could to make an honest woman of her.

At their second shooting party that winter, as she stood by the fireplace talking to James Buckley before lunch, conscious of the efforts of a man called Sir Reginald Farquharson to move closer in their direction, it came to her more forcibly than ever that, because of the situation in which she found herself, she had joined the ranks of those females who were as different from the kind of women whom men like Sir Reginald chose for wives as chalk from cheese. She became depressed and, as soon as lunch was over, made an excuse not to accompany the guns as they trooped out for the afternoon drives.

When Harvey had said goodbye to the last guest that evening, coming back into the drawing-room obviously well pleased, not only with the day's bag but his own performance, she felt quite unable to share his feelings. Suddenly he asked, "What happened which prevented you from coming out this afternoon? Weren't you feeling well? I thought you seemed to be enjoying yourself before lunch. I noticed Reginald Farquharson was especially charming to you—that is, when he was able to get the chance."

She shrugged. "I'm all right. I just didn't feel like going out again. As a matter of fact, I don't think I like watching all that slaughter."

He remained silent. That night he did not come to the tower suite and this time it was she who became scared. She knew she had hurt him. Putting on a dressing-gown and slippers, she did something she had never done before. She went down the steps to his bedroom, opened the door and moved swiftly across to his bed.

"Rose!"

He sat up instantly. She put out a hand. To her relief, he did not reject it. He simply said, "I think it would be better if you went away, back to the tower."

"I came to say I was sorry. I know how much shooting means to you."

There was a longer pause during which she stood motionless, a slim ethereal figure in the moonlit room, her hair hanging loose on her shoulders, her features indistinct except for the enormous eyes with their curious mixture of dependence yet power.

"Go back," he suddenly said again. This time there was a husky tone in his voice. She left him at once, knowing that he would follow. Soon, she heard his footsteps on the stairs.

There were no more disagreements between them that winter. Rose made a point of playing the perfect hostess at all Harvey's subsequent shoots. She even managed to have a brief conference with Mrs Robson before each of them, concerning the kind of food which was to be served. At first the housekeeper openly resented such overtures, but when Rose had been able to tell her how much Sir Reginald Farquharson enjoyed her steak and kidney pudding and warn her that because a rather frail guest was expected next time it might be as well to have an alternative fish dish, the atmosphere seemed to thaw. Mrs Robson was not the only one to realise that, if Rose could have been granted proper status she would make an excellent mistress of Wilcot, not just of the man with whom she had thrown in her lot. All the visitors who came there knew it also. No one could fault Rose's manner or her appearance. Dressed in well-cut tweeds and brogue shoes, standing beside Harvey or one of the other guns at some drive, presiding at lunch or at tea, all that she lacked was a wedding ring, something which, as Christmas drew near and the abdication crisis deepened, she knew would almost certainly soon be possessed by Mrs Wallis Simpson.

It was not until the end of January when the shooting season was over and she and Harvey began spending much more time in their new London home, that trouble between them flared up again. Most of Harvey's energies now seemed to be taken up with a big property deal concerning a substantial area of Notting Hill. Typing some of the reports and letters about this, Rose had been astounded—even alarmed—at the enormity of the sums of money involved. But she knew better than to refer to it. Often, such business kept Harvey out of the house most of the day and she would find herself at a loose end. The very nature of her situation seemed to preclude her from having girl friends and, although in London life was more exciting than in the country, yet it was something for which she was almost entirely dependent on Harvey—and Harvey, at the moment, was too tired and preoccupied of an evening to do much socialising. At Wilcot, she was at least able to enjoy the garden, take the dogs for a walk and interest herself in the village and its inhabitants, even if, as yet, it was only from the point of view of an onlooker.

Sometimes, nowadays, when she was feeling particularly bored or lonely, she would take herself off to a cinema or an art show and it was on one of these latter occasions that she ran into Stephen Forman.

"Rose! Darling! How lovely to see you. Where is Harvey? Surely he doesn't let such a vision go round *unescorted*?"

She laughed. "Sometimes. He's very busy just now."

"Really? More property deals? Dear Harvey has the Midas touch, all right. All the same. . ." He stood back, his eyes giving her a wicked appraisal. "You know, I'm never quite sure what kind of tripe I've written in the tabloids, but in *your* case, my bit about *Portrait of Rose* came from the heart. I believe I said something about allure, not full awareness of it, didn't I? Do you know, I think . . . maybe . . . you have more of both now."

She found herself blushing, furiously, but he appeared not to notice. Taking her arm, he continued, "Darling Rose. Are you on your way home? Please allow me the privilege of taking you in a taxi."

As they reached Number 18—a large imposing white house situated, as its neighbours, in a quiet crescent, he made it plain that he expected to be asked in. "I'd love to see your new abode. You haven't given a house-warming party yet, have you?"

"No. As a matter of fact, we were thinking of doing so sometime in March, but until Harvey's got his new enterprise under way we've rather stalled on fixing a date. It's all taking longer than we thought. And of course, what with having had so many structural alterations done and being down in the country so much there just hasn't been an opportunity before."

She went a little ahead of him and got out her key. Once inside, she said, "I'll ask Corbett to make us some tea, that is, unless you'd prefer something stronger?"

"Tea would be fine, thank you. Contrary to what most people seem to imagine, I'm quite an abstemious sort of chap."

A little later, when she was pouring him out a cup in the drawing-room, he asked, "Where is the celebrated portrait? Is it in one of your other state rooms?"

"As a matter of fact, it's upstairs in my sitting-room."

He raised an eyebrow. "Oh. So it's only on permanent view to its subject?"

"Well, yes. If you put it like that."

There was a short pause in their conversation. Suddenly,

she said, "Would you like to see it again?"

"Yes. I'd like that very much."

They were seated on her small chintz-covered sofa looking at it when Harvey walked in. There was nothing wrong with what they were doing. They were behaving with the utmost propriety. Stephen had been leaning forward slightly, studying the portrait intently. It was perhaps unfortunate that, just as the door opened, he had turned the same attentive gaze on Rose herself, as if comparing the animate and inanimate article.

"Good evening." Rose noticed the habitual frown on Harvey's face deepen as he came across the room. She stood up, far more quickly than Stephen, unable to control the flush to which she invariably succumbed either from pleasure or embarrassment. Just now, it was clearly caused by the latter.

"Rose has been showing me Scholte's masterpiece again," Stephen said. His manner was entirely casual.

"Yes. So I can see."

"I think it's the best thing he's ever done—or likely to."

"Yes." Harvey's own tone of voice made Stephen's next remark almost inevitable.

"Well, I must be getting along. Thank you very much for the tea, Rose." He held out his hand. Rarely had he felt more sorry for anyone. And then, as Harvey made a move towards the door, he added, "Please don't bother to come down. I can see my own way out."

In a few seconds they heard the front door slam.

"I should be obliged in future, Rose," Harvey said, and this time his voice was unnaturally quiet, although the words seemed to reverberate in the silent room long after he had left her, "if you would ensure that your own suite in this house is used for entertaining ladies only."

6

The Buckleys' daughter, Susan, was sixteen and a half at the time of King George VI's coronation that May. She was a pale, thin, painfully shy girl, although there was about her a suppressed eagerness, not unlike the woman she adored from afar. For to Susan, Rose Delafield epitomised all that she most wanted to be: beautiful, sophisticated, exquisitely-dressed and charming. Moreover, Susan had overheard her mother once mentioning that Rose wore *black* in the evening. Susan thought that if she ever became the possessor of a black evening gown she would expire with happiness.

She had never had much contact with her idol. Anne Buckley saw to that. But since the day when Harvey Frayne had called unexpectedly to see James, and Anne had felt obliged to ask his chauffeuse indoors also, Susan had formed what the girls at her day-school in Fordingham called a crush on the older woman. From that time on, she thought of Rose daily, remembered the gorgeous scent she had been wearing—never having heard its name she was quite unaware that it was Chanel Number Five, nor that Harvey was the constant supplier—kept watch for a glimpse of Rose passing through the village and, on one never-to-be-forgotten occasion, found herself occupying the next cubicle to her idol at the Fordingham hairdressers, where Susan was being granted the rare treat of having her hair specially washed and set for the Pony Club Dance.

For many months Anne Buckley knew nothing of her daughter's infatuation. She had become rather too involved with a variety of voluntary activities, which took up a great deal of her time. She was President of the Women's Institute, on a fund-raising committee to provide Wilcot with a new village hall and a member of another committee, which was ambitiously planning an afternoon pageant and a torchlight procession to celebrate the coronation. That her daughter was to be cast as one of Robin Hood's merry men, dressed in green and riding her pony alongside several of her school friends—for it was always the girls who were the more active in the equestrian world—seemed to Anne entirely appropriate until, having missed one of the meetings through influenza, she discovered that Rose Delafield had been chosen to play the part of Maid Marion.

"I don't understand it, James," she said to her husband one night. "What on earth does she think she's doing? Who could possibly have put her name forward? That fool of a rector, I suppose. Tristram Courtenay can never look further than his nose. Anyway, why does Harvey Frayne want to have anything to do with the local celebrations? It's not as if he's here all that much. Why doesn't he stay up in London on May 12th, instead of letting his fancy lady make an exhibition of herself?"

Harvey would, indeed, have preferred to have kept right out of all the shenanigans. The trouble was that Rose did not. She was almost childlike in her pleasure at being asked to play Maid Marion and, in all fairness, Harvey had to admit to himself that it might not be politic to refuse such an invitation. Without showing it, he was just as anxious as Rose that she should be accepted in the neighbourhood.

"They want me to ride sidesaddle," she informed him on returning from a walk, during which she had met the rector who had immediately given her advance warning of the proposal.

"But can you?"

"Well, I never have, but it can't be all that difficult. Apparently my horse will be led by some henchman. And I did a little riding as a child. On a friend's pony. I got quite keen only . . . there was never any money for proper lessons. . ." Her voice trailed away. He noticed her look down at her silk-stockinged legs and fashionable new walking-shoes with the smart tongues. Mutely, she raised her eyes to his and he felt, just at that moment, he could have given her anything.

"I'm sure you'll make a splendid Maid Marion," was all he said. The matter was settled.

But what neither Harvey, nor Rose, nor Anne Buckley had

bargained for was the fact it was James Buckley's aged mare which was considered the most suitable mount for Rose and, as some practice would be necessary, she would be paying several visits to the Buckley household.

Susan, of course, was in ecstasies. That she was actually able to *help* Rose to perform her destined role made it almost impossible for her to talk about anything else. Anne Buckley became furious.

"I can't imagine why you've allowed yourself to be so carried away by Miss Delafield and this pageant," she said, one day. "Don't forget, you're meant to be swatting for School Certificate. You're never going to pass it at this rate."

"But I've always done my homework. And Rose only comes over at weekends. You talk as if you don't like her."

Anne Buckley hesitated. It seemed extraordinary that this daughter of hers, so bright and talented in other ways, was evidently still so naïve that she saw nothing odd about the fact that Rose and Harvey were not married. Possibly, Anne thought, she herself was to blame. She had shrunk from talking to Susan about the facts of life. Living as they did on a farm, she supposed the girl was aware of certain biological facts, yet she seemed totally unaware that Rose could be anything other than a secretary to her employer.

"I've nothing against her personally, Susan," she replied, at length. "I just don't think Miss Delafield and I have anything in common."

"But Daddy seems to get on well with her. He came out and watched when we were practising in Great Croft the other day. He and Rose had quite a long conversation. She was saying how she used to ride when she was growing up in a rectory in East Anglia."

"Yes, maybe. Incidentally, did she ask you to call her by her christian name?"

"Yes."

Anne Buckley pursed her lips. She did not like the situation at all, especially the child's remark about her father. Anne knew well enough that Rose had intrigued and captivated most of the men in the district and that her own husband was not immune to her charms, however faithful a type he was.

Now, it seemed, her own daughter had fallen under the spell. There was something unhealthy about it. She was determined to put an end to the association as soon as the coronation was over.

But for the moment a kind of fever appeared to have overtaken the entire neighbourhood, a fever which, in some extraordinary way, had percolated as far as London. One night the telephone rang at the Grange and Carl Scholte came on the line.

"Harvey? This coronation. I feel I'd like to portray it in some way. You mentioned last time we met that Wilcot was doing the thing in style. I wondered if Elena and I could come down. I could make sketches. Perhaps some of Rose as this Maid Marion."

"Well, yes." The request was almost impossible to refuse, although Harvey was not at all sure he wanted Rose painted again. Sometimes he regretted having allowed her to sit for her portrait in the first place.

"We'd only stay a couple of nights," Carl went on. "I just want to catch the atmosphere and then come straight back to town and get to work."

It was finally arranged that the Scholtes would arrive on the 11th. This time Rose had no fears about their visit. They might be married themselves, but she knew they had plenty of friends living together who were not. In the particular milieu in which they moved, no eyebrows were raised at a liaison such as that between her and Harvey. The fact that it was the source of continual gossip and condemnation in and around Wilcot would have astounded them, had they known. But as they rarely spent more than a few days out of London, the old-fashioned conventional outlook and strange indefinable nuances pertaining to country life passed them by. They were not only foreigners to England. They were foreigners to life as lived in the Shires.

When, a few days before the coronation, Harvey received an urgent telephone call from France requesting his presence because his wife was thought to be dying, Rose was by no means alarmed at the prospect of entertaining the Scholtes by herself, nor, indeed of remaining at Wilcot and going through with the pageant alone. She tried to suppress the thought, but the possibility that Harvey might soon be free to marry sent her spirits soaring. He might have once intimated that he was not, under any circumstances, a marrying man, but she felt reasonably confident that she could force the issue if he actually became a widower. Sh knew that he could not do without her any more than she could do without him. The balance of power between them was well matched. If ever she became fearful, as occasionally after a quarrel, that she might have to become some ordinary secretary living in some dreary bed-sitting-room, the prospect seemed so appalling that, before the day was out, she would succeed in putting things right. She would wear a dress for dinner which she knew Harvey liked, allow herself to come close to him wearing a little extra Chanel Number Five, or perhaps—as if by accident—touch his hand when passing him something. Rose Delafield, the once demure parson's daughter, had come a long way.

She was about to try on her costume for the pageant on the afternoon of the eleventh when Mrs Robson tapped at her bedroom door to say that she was wanted on the telephone. She was surprised to hear Elena's voice because she was due to meet the Scholtes at Fordingham station in a few hours and imagined they might already be on their way.

"Darlink? Such luck. We haf no need to travel by beastly train. We are getting an unexpected lift. Stephen Forman will drive us down in his beautiful old Hispano-Suiza."

"*Stephen Forman?*"

"Yes Darlink. He telephone just now to say he is going to Cornwall. What could be better? We will arrive a little later. Say, seven o'clock, if that is all right. It *is* all right, isn't it, Darlink? You don't sound too 'appy about it."

"Yes. No. I mean, it's quite all right. It's just . . . well, I was surprised, that's all."

"I'm sorry, Darlink. Carl and I . . . we always do so much on spur of moment. I don't know 'ow you feel about this but perhaps Stephen could haf dinner at Wilcot?"

"Yes, of course."

"Good. We'll be seeing you, then."

Rose put down the receiver. How was she going to explain this to Harvey? He would think she had engineered the whole thing. Since the day he had found Stephen and herself alone in her sitting-room, he had never mentioned his name again except that, when they were compiling a list for a house-warming party, he had said, "I suppose we should send an invitation to Forman, but I don't think he'll be able to come. He's in America."

Afterwards, she had wondered whether Harvey had had this in mind when choosing a date for the occasion. Yet could he *possibly* have thought that there had been anything between her and Stephen? Surely not. She found his attitude regrettable yet, at the same time, it gave her a strange excitement to know that she could arouse such jealousy.

It was almost with defiance that she got ready that evening to receive her guests, putting on a smart black ankle-length chiffon dress which was, perhaps, more suited to town than country. But she was able to justify her choice of garment to herself on the grounds that all the visitors were from London. *And Harvey was away.* She was beginning to enjoy a sense of freedom. She could do what she liked. After all, she was in charge at Wilcot, wasn't she?

The car swung into the forecourt at exactly seven p.m., while she was standing at the drawing-room window. She heard Robson open the front door and then voices—mostly Elena's. She went out into the hall to welcome them all.

"Darlink!" Elena came towards her, arms outstretched, and kissed her on both cheeks.

"Rose, my dear!" Carl immediately followed suit.

"Rose!" Stephen Forman held out his hand and she shook it, almost formally.

"Darlink! I did not know. This Stephen. He drives like a maniac. I haf terrible 'eadache. Would you mind if I go straight to bed?" Elena already had one eye on the staircase.

"No. Not at all. We'll send your dinner up on a tray."

"Darlink. How kind. Such a good hostess. But only a very leetle, mind."

Elena, Carl and Robson disappeared and she was left alone with Stephen.

"It's nice of you," he said, when they were having a drink in the drawing-room, awaiting the reappearance of Carl, "to be giving me dinner. I must say I feel privileged to see Harvey's country seat and catch a glimpse of you as chatelaine in another setting. Tell me, which *modus vivendi* do you like best?"

It was not a figure of speech with which she was acquainted, but she knew well enough what he meant.

"It's hard to say," she replied. "I suppose I understand this one best, having been brought up in the country. But . . . well, London often seems easier."

"Easier?"

"Yes. Socially. I mean. . ." The word had slipped out. She realised that she had acknowledged her doubtful status, that she was treating Stephen as a confidant, something she had never done before with anyone.

He nodded, obviously not at all surprised. "I hope," he said, "that you don't let the conventional dyed-in-the-wool Conservative matrons round here get you down."

She laughed. "Not really. At least I've been asked to take part in the coronation festivities."

"I wish I could stay and join in, too," he answered, and she knew that he meant it.

He repeated the words when she wished him goodbye that night. Carl had taken himself off to bed immediately after dinner, saying that he did not want to disturb Elena once she had gone to sleep; but Stephen had stayed on drinking several more cups of coffee in order to fortify himself—as he said—for the long drive ahead. At last, reluctantly, round about eleven, he got up to go and she came out into the forecourt to see him off. The scent of hay was overpowering in the night air. In the lake below them, the reflection of the moon was as bright as the huge white orb shining above. Away to the right a few squares of orange light showed through the trees, proclaiming that not all the inhabitants of Wilcot were asleep. From the direction of the kennels at the back of the house, a dog barked. On the opposite side of the valley, where the celebratory bonfire was to be lit, the outline of the downs showed black and somehow slightly menacing. She shivered, slightly.

"You're cold, my sweet." The term of endearment had slipped out, just as something she had said about her own status had done earlier that evening.

He put a hand under each of her elbows.

"Dearest Rose." He leant forward and kissed her, very gently, on the lips. Then, for good measure, he repeated the procedure with much more ardour.

7

Underneath the spreading chestnut tree, I loved her and she loved me . . . sang the crooner at a charity ball in aid of Fordingham's local hospital.

From where he was sitting, dressed in white tie and tails, Harvey Frayne watched the scene in front of him, an expression of boredom, almost distaste, on his face. The words seemed so utterly banal, the antics of the dancers quite ridiculous. Somewhere in the throng he could see Rose, wearing a glamorous Norman Hartnell creation of pale blue silk—a colour much favoured by the new Queen that year— obviously enjoying herself enormously, as she cavorted about with a red-faced perspiring Reginald Farquharson.

Although Harvey had been more than willing to buy tickets for the occasion—generously adding an extra nought to his cheque—he had not actually intended putting in an appearance himself. But when, during a chance encounter, Reginald had suggested that they might all meet up, he had given in, partly because he realised that to be seen in public with the Farquharsons would be socially advantageous, partly because it would please Rose. He supposed, now, that he ought to ask the woman sitting beside him to dance, but he felt it would be better to wait until the band struck up something more decorous, such as a slow fox-trot. The idea of Mildred Farquharson and himself making an exhibition of themselves, pretending to be spreading chestnuts or whatever it was everyone else thought they were doing, was too awful to contemplate.

Harvey felt that probably much the same thought had also occurred to his companion. She was a small nondescript-looking woman, whom he suspected was only there on sufferance. Left to herself, Harvey did not imagine that Mildred would risk being seen hobnobbing with a couple over whom he was well aware hung an unfortunate question mark; but having spent a lifetime deferring to the wishes of her large ebullient husband, all she could now do was to sit back and watch him behave like a complete fool. For it seemed to Harvey there was no doubt that it was Rose's undeniable sex appeal—a combination of apparent innocence yet flirtatiousness—which had brought the four of them together that evening. As he watched her and Reginald return, flushed, from the dance-floor, Harvey wondered how much Mildred minded, how much, over the years, she had had to put up with her husband's susceptible nature. He also wondered just how much Rose was aware or unaware of what she could do to a man. He was determined to take her to task about her behaviour as soon as possible.

He raised the matter that very night when they were back at Wilcot enjoying a nightcap in the drawing-room before retiring. On handing her a glass, it came to him as something of a shock to realise that a year ago it would have contained squash only. Now she asked for a gin and orange.

He watched her standing with one arm resting along the mantelshelf, the blue perfectly fitting dress, with its fluted fish-tail frills at the bottom, hugging her slim figure, her auburn hair, which she now wore in a fashionable page-boy bob, slightly disordered, her eyes bright, almost triumphant.

"Such fun," she said. "I so enjoyed tonight." And then, when he did not immediately reply, she continued, "Didn't you?"

"No."

"I'm sorry." She took another sip of her drink.

"Rose," he said. "I think you should take care. It is one thing to play the charming hostess when Reginald comes here to shoot. Quite another to flirt with him in public."

"Flirt?" The enormous eyes opened wider.

"What else were you doing?"

"Just . . . having fun."

He turned away. "I don't think it was much fun for Mildred."

"Oh. I'm sorry."

"Reginald is a married man." He could have bitten the words back, but it was too late. Along with many another development, Rose was beginning to be uncomfortably quick at repartee.

"So are you."

There was silence. The clock in the stable yard struck three. He knew how disappointed Rose had been—even though, to her credit, she had done her best to hide it—when his wife had pulled round earlier that year after being at death's door. This animated young woman before him, however much she might be enjoying an ever-growing confidence in her dealings with the opposite sex, so obviously craved respectability. If Thora had died, would he, Harvey wondered, have broken his vow never to marry again? In order to keep Rose, he believed now that the answer would have been yes. He realised that he was not being fair, that he was asking the impossible not only of Rose but of society itself. It had occurred to him that it was possible she might even want a child, although she had never hinted at that. Sometimes he felt that he did not really know her at all.

He turned away, his emotions confused, the only certain one being that he would like to take Rose to bed, that her power over him was as great or greater than on the day when he had first caught sight of her. It amounted, he supposed, to a weakness in him. She had become an obsession. He felt if he lost her he might do something desperate. He did not think he had all that much to worry about when it came to men like Reginald Farquharson. But there was another type. Stephen Forman, for instance. He was young, different, strikingly good-looking and amusing. Harvey believed and hoped he had put an end to that little association. Or had he? He did not think that Rose had seen Stephen since the time when, presumably in all innocence, she had entertained him in her sitting-room.

Rose had actually kept meaning to tell Harvey about Stephen's visit to Wilcot, but somehow the opportunity for *casually* bringing this into their conversation never seemed to arise. As the weeks passed, she had decided to leave well alone. She was aware that at some future date the subject might crop up, that the Scholtes themselves might mention it. But, with almost childlike ingenuousness, she hoped by then that sufficient time would have elapsed for it not to matter.

She knew that she should never have allowed Stephen to kiss her in the way he had, nor to have responded in like manner, but she had managed to push the memory to the back of her mind. She had not seen him since and imagined he was in the States, as he had vaguely intimated on parting. She was totally unprepared for Harvey's sudden remark as she drove him back to town on the Monday following the hospital ball.

"Haven't seen anything of Forman lately, have we?"

"No." She had been about to overtake a lorry, but now she slowed. She realised that it was time to take care in more ways than one.

"He seems to have giving up writing his usual art column. I suppose he's abroad or something."

"Yes. I expect so."

Could she, should she, say more? How would she put it? "By the way, I forgot to tell you, Stephen had dinner at Wilcot when you were in France. He was driving down to Cornwall and gave the Scholtes a lift." But she had not forgotten. How could she? And Harvey would know that.

She hesitated, just a fraction too long. The moment was lost, although Harvey's next words made her more uneasy than ever. Was it merely coincidence that he now referred to the very occasion uppermost in her mind?

"Come to think of it, we haven't seen anything of the Scholtes either," he said. "I must ring Carl up when we get to London. I'm surprised he hasn't wanted to show us the result of his work at Wilcot. Did he make sketches of you as Maid Marion, as he intended?"

"Yes. But only as part of a general scene, along with the Buckleys' daughter and several others."

"I should think the girl would like to see them."

"Yes." Rose did not add that Susan had asked her about this only the other day when they had met in the village. She was beginning to find the sixteen-year-old's abject devotion to her as irritating and worrying as she knew it to be to Susan's mother.

If it had not been for her feelings of guilt, Rose would have been all for getting in touch with the Scholtes long before now. She had, in fact, been both disappointed and surprised at

Carl's silence. For over a year, she had secretly gloated over her portrait and the public's reaction to it. Since its appearance, an insidious narcissism seemed to have crept up on her. She spent more and more time before the mirror, more and more of Harvey's money on her clothes. She could not help sometimes wondering what it would be like to be made love to by another man. But she was shrewd enough to realise that if her present way of life was to continue, there must never be a repetition of anything approaching her and Stephen's amorous farewell.

To her relief, the Scholtes were just off to Greece when Harvey telephoned them the following day. Elena explained that Carl had not been at all well and his painting had suffered in consequence. He had become acutely depressed by the international situation and felt sure there would be another war. She was hoping a holiday might help him.

For twenty-four hours, Rose felt as if she had had a reprieve. Then, when Harvey was out, she answered the telephone to hear Stephen's voice on the line.

"Rose, darling. Please forgive me. I never wrote to thank you for all your delicious hospitality back in May. It was unforgivable of me. I've no excuse, except that writing for a living tends to make one a hopeless correspondent."

"But there was absolutely no need. How was New York?"

"Hot."

She wondered what was coming next.

"Darling, I've got to go to Essex to interview an elderly chap who does etchings. I thought . . . well, if you aren't doing anything tomorrow you might care to come along. It would make all the difference to have the pleasure of your company."

"Oh." She was completely taken aback. Was Stephen mad? It was such a preposterous idea. Surely he must have realised it was out of the question. Yet she knew that in the circles in which the Scholtes and Stephen lived it was not so strange, in the same way as addressing her as 'Darling' was nothing more than a mannerism. After all, Elena was often seen with some male companion or other when Carl was busy. No one thought anything of it. But then, even if they had not been married,

Carl and Elena were different. They belonged to another
world. They were a devoted couple who could each afford to
have friends of the opposite sex. She and Harvey were
somehow not a couple; they were not really anything. They
were two people who, much as Rose shied away from the
expression, were living in sin, at any rate as far as the
inhabitants of Wilcot and the surrounding neighbourhood
looked at it. For the privilege of being the mistress of a man
who was by no means an artist, but who aspired to be a
country gentleman—one who kept her constantly supplied
with all the material luxuries for which any woman could
possibly ask—she was obliged to behave as more married than
the married.

"I'm sorry, Stephen," she faltered, "but. . ."

"All right, darling. You don't need to say more. I
understand. But you mustn't let yourself become too much of
a prisoner."

8

The typed letter in its buff envelope awaiting Rose on the breakfast table at Wilcot came as a surprise. It seemed on the large side for any bill from a fashion house, the kind of item which accounted for most of her post nowadays. She opened it quickly and glanced through its content.

"Oh, *no!*"

"What is it, Rose?" Harvey lowered *The Times*.

"It's . . . Aunt Jackson. This is from her solicitor. She's died. Out in Cairo."

"I'm sorry."

Rose re-read the missive, this time more slowly. "Dear Miss Delafield," it ran,

I regret to have to inform you that your aunt, Mrs Isobel Jackson, passed away two weeks ago in Cairo, where she had been suffering from dysentery.

I am enclosing a copy of her Will, from which you will note that she has left you a legacy of one hundred pounds and the choice of any one of her paintings. Apart from a few other minor bequests, you will also note that her residual estate goes to an artists' benevolent fund.

Perhaps you would care to write or telephone me so that we could make a mutually convenient appointment for you to see your aunt's work and make your selection.

      Yours sincerely,
      John Berridge

She passed the letter over to Harvey. It was difficult to think of Aunt Jackson as dead. She had always been such a positive, alive sort of person. How ghastly it must have been for her to have been ill and dying all alone in a foreign country. What sort of hospital had she been in, Rose wondered. Had she had proper medical attention? Probably not. That was why she

51

had died. She had always had such a tough constitution.

When Harvey handed the letter back to her, she was aware of a curious expression on his face.

"I suppose your aunt felt that you were well provided for."

She stared at him. "How do you mean?"

"Has it never occurred to you to think about your future . . . if anything happens to me?"

She flushed. It was true that she knew she enjoyed a high standard of living, for which a certain price had to be paid; but she had never given much thought to what would happen when Harvey died or, if she had, she had vaguely imagined he would have made some sort of provision for her. Wills and death were not subjects which came into her scheme of things. She was young. The way ahead seemed endlessly pleasurable. It was impossible to imagine growing old, acquiring wrinkles like Mildred Farquharson. She was sometimes conscious that Harvey was ageing. She did not connect that process with herself.

When she did not answer his question, he continued, "Naturally, I have taken your position into account. Half of my estate will pass to my wife and daughter, half to you."

"Oh". She became flustered. Then, because her response seemed somehow inadequate, she added, "Thank you."

He came with her to view her aunt's paintings on the day which was eventually agreed upon. Being already interested in the arts, it seemed a perfectly reasonable thing for him to do and she was, in fact, glad of a little support. But she could not help thinking she might have preferred to be accompanied by Stephen Forman. As it turned out she found herself accepting Harvey's advice to choose a picture of an African negress. On her own, she felt she would have preferred to opt for a very early water-colour of the Norfolk rectory where she was brought up.

"The picture of the negress has power," Harvey said, after they had said goodbye to Mr Berridge. "You may well find that your aunt acquires a posthumous reputation. I should say it is the most valuable in the whole collection."

She remained silent. She did not want the most valuable in Aunt Jackson's collection. What was more, she was puzzled and distressed that, with all Harvey's money, he seemed so keen for her to have it. She wondered what would have happened had she been with Stephen. More and more, she found herself thinking about him nowadays. She had no intention of seeing him privately, but she felt it would have been nice to meet on some purely social occasion.

In this her wish was granted. Towards Christmas that year, the Scholtes invited Rose and Harvey to dinner. "Quite informal, Darlink, you understand," Elena had said on the telephone. "Carl is better but he must not do too much. We only plan to have one other couple, Frank Henderson, you know, the man who owns the Frejus gallery, and the woman who helps him to run it, Gillian Lamonte."

Rose flipped through the engagement diary. "I think we should love to come," she replied. "We're spending quite a lot of time at Wilcot just now because of the shooting, but I know Harvey has to be in London that week for some important meetings."

Rose was delighted to have received such an invitation. While life at Wilcot was often preferable in the summer, she was beginning to find being there in the winter distinctly trying. Harvey's preoccupation with shooting depressed her. It had become something of a strain pretending to be interested, forcing herself to say, as the guns trooped in for lunch, that she hoped they had had a "good" morning, and then listening to the figures of the slaughtered birds discussed over steak and kidney pudding. She felt herself to be a complete hypocrite, constantly acting out a role of which she did not approve. At least in London she could enjoy more anonymity, even if she was increasingly unsure how to fill in her time since, for several months, Harvey had engaged the services of an elderly spinster, a Miss Tetley, to do his secretarial work.

"I don't feel," he had said one night in an unexpected burst of confidence and tenderness, "that you should do any more of this kind of thing. You are . . ." and here he had cleared his throat and looked embarrassed, "well . . . much more to me than . . . a secretary. That room in the basement next to the Corbetts' flat can be made into an office. Miss Tetley needn't even come into the house. She can go down the area steps and be let in that way. It might not be advisable to say too much about all this at Wilcot, but I shall simply tell Chapman to arrange for any office work to be done in his own home. I rather think his wife was a typist before they married."

Rose had been astonished, firstly by what amounted to be an admission of love, secondly by the realisation that Harvey was definitely putting their relationship on a different footing. On the strength of it, she had gone out and bought an emerald green tea-gown, which had completely taken Harvey aback when he had found her wearing it the following afternoon. For a moment, he wondered if the moves he had proposed were wise ones. But, noting the instant and almost childlike pleasure which they seemed to have given, he felt perhaps they were worth it.

He knew how little it took to raise Rose's spirits, to see the sudden look of wonderment come over her face. When he saw what the prospect of dining with the Scholtes meant to her, he realised that he had never seen her looking quite so happy since the time when he had told her about Miss Tetley. He had accepted the fact that she had not been enjoying their life at Wilcot so much of late, although he was unaware of the extent of her dislike of shooting. He had no intention of cutting down on his sporting activities but, when possible, he was anxious to make it up to her in other ways. For this reason, he had bought some surprise theatre tickets and was intending to take her to a Rattigan play, *French Without Tears*, the evening after Carl and Elena's party.

When Harvey succumbed to influenza during the weekend before they were due back in London, Rose, though disappointed, made every effort to encourage him to stay at Wilcot and cancel all his engagements. But he refused to alter any of his plans. He explained that the business meetings were vital and he was determined to carry on regardless which, in so far as going to London and attending his first meeting were concerned, he did. But at five o'clock that day it was all he could do to crawl into bed. Rose was all prepared for a quiet evening at home when, to her surprise, Harvey insisted that she should go alone.

"You were so looking forward to it, my dear," he said, when she came up to ask if he would like a cup of tea. "I've telephoned Carl and they would be delighted to have you. If I take care tonight, I'll probably be quite recovered by tomorrow."

With misgiving, she dressed for the dinner party and left him. On arrival, she found her host and hostess had arranged a stopgap.

"Darling Rose," said Stephen, rising to greet her as she entered the room, "what a sight for sore eyes . . ."

9

They would only stay an hour, Stephen promised her. After all, the Café de Paris was only a little way out of their way. And the party had broken up so early, because of Carl's health. Surely she would like to dance, wouldn't she? Harvey had obviously wanted her to have some fun. Otherwise he wouldn't have urged her to go out without him. He couldn't possibly object to her prolonging the evening a little longer.

Stephen's persuasive manner was difficult to resist. Sitting beside him in his old Hispano-Suiza as they sped away from Hampstead, she made less and less attempt to do so. Carl and Elena were generous hosts and she had drunk more than usual—more, in fact, than Stephen, who was simply being his usual charming inconsequential self.

And if they really only stayed an hour, Harvey need never know, Rose said to herself. She would have to tell him Stephen had been there, of course, and that he had brought her home. But it was purely accidental that the Scholtes had asked him as a stopgap on the spur of the moment and, considering the kind of life he led, quite remarkable that he had happened to be free. And she would so love to dance. Harvey never danced, unless one could count his laboured efforts at the hospital ball.

Long before they arrived at the Café de Paris, she had given up any attempt at preventing her and Stephen's little escapade. It seemed somehow inevitable. She could hardly wait to take to the dance-floor. If, in the ladies' cloakroom, a still small voice said, "What are you doing? Are you mad?" she stifled it. She was a creature of the moment. Play now. Pay later.

As she had suspected, Stephen proved to be a superb dancer. Owing to the rather strange life she had led, Rose had never had much opportunity for dancing, but such was her partner's proficiency and her own natural talent that she soon found they made a perfect couple, as tune followed tune: *Night and Day*, *These Foolish Things* and *Let's Do It*. By one a.m. she was as drunk on dancing as she was on the champagne with which she was being plied.

It was Stephen who reminded her of the time. "I think we should go, my sweet, much as I should like to stay here all night."

"Oh, yes. Yes, of course."

He made no attempt to kiss her when he drew up outside Number 18. As he ran round and opened the door of the car, he merely counteracted her thanks by saying, "It is I who must thank you. I've often found that the most pleasurable things in life are unplanned."

Then he escorted her up the steps, waited as she turned her key in the lock and was gone, his Hispano-Suiza roaring away into the London night.

She closed the front door softly, hoping not to wake Harvey. Gathering up her long, rather tight skirt, she walked slowly up the wide circular staircase. It was not until she was almost at the top that she saw him standing silently by the door leading to his own apartment at the far end of the landing. She faltered, almost tripping on the last step.

"I telephoned the Scholtes," he said, as she came towards him, "at eleven thirty. They said you and Stephen Forman had left their house half an hour before and you should be back any minute. It is now one forty-five."

Fear and a certain muzziness kept her silent. She felt like a child being rebuked by a tyrannical parent, except that the man before her was no parent. Despite the lateness of the hour and the alcohol she had drunk, she suddenly saw him for what he was: an ageing lover, on whom she was utterly dependent, now half-crazed by jealousy. His usually sallow complexion was suffused by two bright red splashes on either cheekbone. His eyes glittered. She knew that his feverish state must have something to do with it, but she also suspected that it was she who was really responsible for his extraordinary, even terrifying, appearance.

"Well? Where have you been?"

It could have been stern Victorian father interrogating

wayward daughter.

"I . . . we . . . went to the Café de Paris."

"A *night-club!*"

"Yes, Harvey, please. . ." It suddenly came to her that he had never actually taken her to a night-club. Could it be that in some way he disapproved of them? She put out a hand.

She was quite unprepared for another which came up and hit her across the face. Nor for hearing the word "whore" as he turned and went back to his apartment and closed the door.

For a while she stood there, unable to move, unable to comprehend or believe what had just happened. Then she, too, stumbled to her own rooms. Once there, she went across to a long mirror, partly to reassure herself of her existence, partly because her face was hurting. She was alarmed by the reflection which stared back at her, not so much by the red weal brought about by Harvey's blow, but because of an overall picture of something akin to decadence. The Molyneux dress she had been wearing, though highly fashionable, seemed somehow too tight; her page-boy bob, disordered; the effect of the champagne still evident in her eyes. Was she, in fact, turning into the kind of woman such as Harvey had accused her of being? What had happened to her of late? Memories of her childhood came flooding back: a hazy recollection of a grey-haired harassed mother, a clearer one of the saintly man who had been her father, who had once made that curious remark about the spirit being willing but the flesh weak. Was it possible that he had ever strayed from the straight and narrow after—or even before—her mother's death? Surely not. His words had simply been an observation, a statement, rather like a text for one of his sermons.

But she, his daughter, was different. She had early on fallen from grace. Could she now ever make amends, redeem herself, find some decent ordinary man—not the reckless charmingly irresponsible kind she knew Stephen Forman to be, much as she was attracted to him—who would marry her? What would such a paragon say if he knew of her past? Would she ever be able to live it down, keep it secret? Hardly. Not now. Besides, she would never have enough courage to leave Harvey, start off on her own. There would be no more luxurious living accommodation such as that in which she was now standing, no more fashionable creations such as the one she was now wearing. Almost involuntarily, she smoothed her hands down over her hips. She couldn't give up all this unless, of course, she was forced to leave. After what had just happened, that result seemed more than likely. As she undressed, letting black satin frock, lace-trimmed black silk cami-knickers and matching brassière fall to the floor, panic overcame her. Pulling on an equally glamorous nightdress, she got into bed, but sleep eluded her, as she tossed about restlessly, wondering what the morning would bring.

To her surprise, it did not bring the further cross-questioning which she had been expecting. Harvey came down to breakfast, now pale and perfectly calm. He announced that he was better, that he would be attending another meeting as arranged and taking her to the theatre that evening. The only reference he made to what had just occurred came as he got up to leave the room. "I think, Rose, that we both have cause to feel sorry about our behaviour last night. Neither of us can afford to let it happen again."

In other words, she thought ruefully, as she heard him go into his study and close the door, as long as she was prepared to toe the line—his line—the subject was closed.

During the following weeks they were wary of each other, as carefully polite and courteous as they had been before they ever became lovers. Harvey, in fact, did not come to her bedroom in either home and she began to wonder whether the sexual side of their relationship was over. But if it were, why did he want her to remain with him? Was he, perhaps, testing her out? She had an uneasy feeling she was on trial, that she was being watched. She would look up suddenly to find him staring at her. She became nervous, doing her best to avoid being with him for any length of time.

It was not until the shooting season was coming to an end and they began spending more time in London after Christmas that Rose felt almost certain that she was being watched, but not only by Harvey. Her "shadow", as she thought of him, was by no means a little man in a bowler hat and shabby raincoat, such as she had read about in novels which touched on divorce. He was a perfectly ordinary-looking member of the public, conventionally dressed in an Anthony Eden trilby and dark overcoat who could easily be taken for a respectable businessman. The first time she became aware of him had been when she had gone by taxi to Whiteleys in Bayswater to buy some trimmings she particularly wanted for a hat being made for her by a new go-ahead young milliner called Ashley Arr. As she paid off her driver at the corner of Queen's Road, he asked her whether she had been aware that another cab had been trailing them throughout the journey and was now stopping at the far end of the street. She frowned, took a quick look at the figure who was alighting and decided that her own cabby was spinning her a yarn. She had actually purchased the feathers and ribbon she required and was about to leave the shop when she suddenly caught sight of the same figure, this time studiously surveying some men's ties.

Could it be, she wondered, that the cab driver had been correct? Or was she being silly even to entertain the idea? It was probably all due to her present heightened nervous state. The man choosing a tie looked like just the kind of man who would be in that kind of shop doing that very thing. Or would he? Would he not have gone to Jermyn Street or Savile Row for his sartorial requirements? And now she came to think of it, she could have sworn that she had noticed him somewhere before. Racking her brains in the taxi back to Belgravia, it suddenly came to her that it had been a week or so ago when Harvey had had to attend a men-only city luncheon. He had enquired at breakfast about her own plans for the day, something he invariably did of late. She had told him that she was thinking of ringing Elena and asking her if she would like to come with her to see Charlie Chaplin in *Modern Times*, for she knew that Harvey, much as he enjoyed the theatre, had rather the same attitude to the cinema as he had towards night clubs.

She recalled him frowning. For a moment she thought he might have been going to veto the idea, however difficult and embarrassing it might be; because since the fatal night when the Scholtes, in all innocence, had roped Stephen in for their dinner party, Rose sensed that Harvey considered them greatly to blame for the situation.

"My luncheon won't take all day," she remembered him saying, slowly. "When do you think you will be home?" And then her reply, "I'm . . . not sure. Five o'clock or thereabouts." She had been utterly astonished when he had said, "I should like to see Elena again. Perhaps you would care to ask her to tea."

Surprise had turned to anger then. He didn't trust her. Presumably he didn't trust Elena. He thought that the idea of going to the pictures was a put-up job, that in some way she would be seeing Stephen that afternoon.

She recalled quite clearly now having seen the man as they went up the steps of the Gaumont. He was looking at his watch, head lowered, giving every indication that he was waiting for a companion. But, during the interval, she had caught sight of him sitting quite alone several rows behind them when she had gone to the cloakroom. She remembered thinking that some lady friend must have let him down and how odd it was that he was no longer there when she returned to her seat.

She had not noticed him again until today, when visiting Whiteleys. On the way back to Number 18 she found herself trembling and more than once taking a furtive look out of the rear window of the cab. What *was* Harvey up to? It wasn't as if they were married and he wished to cite someone else in a divorce case. He did not appear to want her to leave him. Indeed, in many ways he was more attentive than ever. He had taken her to the theatre three times during the previous week. Was it that he was still eaten up with jealousy, terrified of losing her, terrified of letting her out of his sight?

As time passed, she began to feel the prisoner which Stephen had once suggested she might be. Claustrophobia attacked her, particularly whenever they were in London. If she could have done so without arousing suspicion, she would have removed herself from the house more often and simply taken long walks in Hyde Park, especially as spring seemed on its way early that year. It was a definite relief to get back to Wilcot where the atmosphere was less oppressive, where she could walk the dogs without expecting to see a man in an Anthony Eden hat lurking down one of the groves in Folly Woods.

10

One Friday in the middle of March, Rose found Harvey
unusually silent as she drove him back to the west country.
She thought at first that it might be due to his preoccupation
with the news of Hitler's annexation of Austria. Unlike
herself, he took an intense interest in what was happening in
Germany. As far as Rose was concerned, politics bored her,
especially foreign politics. It was a subject best left to the
experts: Neville Chamberlain and his colleagues. She could
not understand why Harvey—or Carl Scholte, for that
matter—took the international situation so seriously. She had
been a baby during the First World War. She could not
envisage another, however much she knew there was real fear
in many people's minds, resulting in air-raid shelters being
dug and mock black-outs taking place.

Later that evening, however, she realised that Harvey's
silence had nothing to do with Germany but all to do with
herself. After dinner—a meal at which he ate hardly
anything—he asked if she would come into his study with
him, a room to which he always went when he particularly did
not want to be disturbed.

Afterwards, she felt that she would always remember the
way he looked just then, as he stood by the fireplace, how
shocked she had been suddenly to notice how much weight he
had lost so that his dinner-jacket hung on him loosely, like a
scarecrow's, how his face was ashen, save for the dark lines
beneath his eyes and running down on either side of his
mouth. His whole appearance gave the impression of an
etching: black and white and strangely still.

"What were you doing," he began, at length, "on the
afternoon of Tuesday last in Kensington Church Street?"

"Kensington Church Street?" she repeated, playing for
time.

"Yes."

She thought back to the occasion. She had gone to Ashley Arr's new establishment which he had just opened opposite Kensington Place. "I went to have a fitting for a hat," she answered, simply.

"But you have just had a hat made."

She coloured. "This was another one. I knew the Royal Academy Private View would be coming along in May and you did mention before . . ."—she hardly liked to say 'the Scholtes' party'—"that you wished you could take me to Ascot, that is if you could somehow have got over the difficulty of obtaining tickets for the Royal Enclosure." She did not add that she had actually ordered three hats.

"Do your fittings normally take over two hours?"

"No."

"Then why did you not return to the house until after five?"

"It was a lovely day. I decided to walk back through Hyde Park."

She could see exactly what had happened. Although she had not noticed her shadow for several days, she had evidently been followed. Ashley's new place was really a large garden flat, and when he had taken her on a tour of the premises, of which he was justly proud, he had shown her out via the patio at the back. From there she had walked straight into the Park. Presumably, by so doing, she had foiled the detective who had been lurking about at the front.

"I suggest," she heard Harvey continue, "that you did no such thing. You merely used this fancy new milliner in order to make an assignation. I have information that he is far from scrupulous and would do anything to advance himself, both socially and financially. Whether you actually met Stephen Forman there or, as I have since discovered, left by another entrance to make your way to Forman's house, is immaterial. You have been unfaithful, Rose, probably for some time."

She was shaking now, fear and anger rendering her speechless. Presently, she managed to burst out, "But I haven't. How dare you have me watched."

"It seemed only natural, my dear, considering your conduct. Can you honestly tell me that you have never seen Forman without my being present, other than the day he brought you home from that art show and the evening before Christmas when you went to the Scholtes?"

She saw now in his eyes something she had long suspected: a hint of madness. She wondered why it had never struck her earlier how abnormal he was, not just in his fanatical desire for money, for power and, it would seem, particularly for her. He was a man possessed and obsessed, so divided within himself that he kept all his various urges in watertight compartments, enabling him to maintain a façade which hid the weakness within. And, because of another kind of weakness in her, she had gone along with him.

"Well?" Still he stood there, waiting for her reply.

She felt perhaps he already knew that Stephen had come to dinner at Wilcot while he had been away in France. If he did, and she lied about it, then in the mood he was in, he looked as if he might kill her. If she admitted it, she might easily suffer the same fate. Either way, she was lost.

"Only once. . ." she faltered. He took a step forward. A hand gripped her wrist and she cried out in agony. He gave her no opportunity to continue. "Only *once?*" he sneered, his face close to hers. "Don't bother to deceive me any more, Rose. Unfortunately, I had not arranged for your movements to be checked when you professed to have gone to the Café de Paris to dance. Had I done so, it is perfectly plain that I should have found you and Stephen Forman had spent the midnight hours at his house by Holland Park."

Then he let go of her, turned and walked out of the room.

She was not conscious of going up to the tower suite that night, only of finding herself, in the early morning, lying on her bed, still fully-clothed, when Mrs Robson brought her early morning tea. Even in her bemused state, Rose wondered why the housekeeper was doing what was usually the job of one of the housemaids.

"Miss Delafield?" The woman stood there, concerned and puzzled.

"Yes?"

Rose propped herself up, distressed to have been caught by Mrs Robson, of all people, in such an obviously questionable state. There was a smudge of lipstick on one of the sleeves of her dinner-gown. She could see her shoes, which she had not bothered to remove, sticking out from under the eiderdown.

"Miss Delafield. We thought you should know," Mrs Robson paused slightly and then went on, "when Robson took up Mr Frayne's tea he found that his bed had not been slept in."

"Not been slept in?"

"No, Miss Delafield. We . . . wondered if anything was wrong. The side door to the garden was unlocked. Robson clearly remembers locking it last night. He is so careful about that sort of thing."

She did not answer. A lot was wrong but she could not tell this woman standing before her, who with admirable self-possession and common sense was now saying, "Perhaps Mr Chapman should be informed." Harvey's manager was invariably referred to as such by the other members of the staff, however much they thought of him as 'Fred' amongst themselves.

"Chapman?" Rose always copied Harvey, when it came to addressing employees.

"Why, yes, Miss Delafield." Mrs Robson remained, as might have been expected even in the middle of a crisis, correct and composed, although Rose sensed that she was becoming a little impatient with her own inadequate responses. "Robson and I thought he could organise a search party in case perhaps . . . Mr Frayne has been taken ill."

"Yes. Yes, I see. Please ring him. I'll be down as soon as possible."

The housekeeper left and she quickly got up and began changing her attire, her mind all at once beginning to race. Should she, herself, have rung the manager? Should the police be informed? Had Harvey disappeared merely in order to frighten her? Yet, strange as he was, it was out of keeping for him to do anything in which the servants might become involved. Perhaps he was really ill, wandering about in some kind of daze. He had never been the same since that bout of influenza which had so unfortunately coincided with their first really serious quarrel. It seemed amazing to realise that she had not noticed how thin he had become.

It was Chapman who brought her the news less than an hour
later. She would like to have joined the searchers, but he had
said that he thought it would be best if she remained indoors.
She was standing by the drawing-room window when she
heard the sound of the small truck he used coming into the
forecourt. She ran to the front door to find him walking
towards her, taking off his cap.

"You've found him?"

He nodded.

"Thank God." Even then, she was somehow totally
unprepared for the information she was about to receive. She
waited, while Chapman looked down, then away, anywhere
but at her until, all at once, as if by a great effort of will, he
stared her straight in the face and, in his deep west country
burr, said, "I am sorry, Miss Delafield. I'm afraid Mr Frayne
. . . is dead."

"*Dead*?" She put out a hand against the stone porch.

"Perhaps . . . you would like to go inside." He helped her
back to the drawing-room and into a chair. She was vaguely
aware of Mrs Robson on the other side of her.

"Where. . .?" she asked.

"In Folly Woods. Down in the Long Grove. An ambulance
has taken him to Fordingham hospital."

"Do you know what it was? A heart attack? Some kind of
stroke?"

There was a long pause. She could hear the sound of voices,
footsteps, the search party returning.

Presently Chapman said, "There was a shot-gun beside
him, Miss Delafield. It could have been an accident."

11

The solicitor who came down from London the following Tuesday was elderly: a small, thin, wizened-looking man called Ernest MacKenzie.

Rose had spent the previous three days in bed and, but for Mrs Robson, would like to have remained there.

"I do not think it would be seemly, Miss Delafield, for you to receive Mr MacKenzie in the tower suite. It will be necessary to give him lunch, having come all that way. I will serve something light. I'm sure we must all do our best in these sad circumstances. It is what Mr Frayne would have wished."

Apart from the Reverend Mr Courtenay, Rose had seen no one from outside since the tragedy, but both the Farquharsons and the Buckleys had left notes of condolence, together with offers of help. Once or twice she had been on the point of telephoning the Scholtes and then, at the last minute, found herself unable to lift the receiver. Moreover, with Carl's health so precarious, she knew there was little they could do, although, before the notice of Harvey's death appeared in *The Times*—which she understood would almost certainly be on Wednesday—she realised, for courtesy's sake she would have to let them know. The person she would like to have rung was Stephen but, in this instance, the knowledge of all that she would be obliged to reveal and explain made it virtually impossible. And the fact that she had not technically been unfaithful to Harvey—however much she might have fantasised about such an event—made the whole situation so much harder to accept.

As he had died at the beginning of a weekend, the normal procedures connected with a death had inevitably been delayed. Fred Chapman had been unable to contact Ernest MacKenzie until the Monday morning. Rose herself, not only in a state of shock but also in an extremely ambiguous position, seemed powerless to give an opinion over the question of telegrams to Harvey's wife, funeral arrangements and so forth. So much depended on the will, which Ernest MacKenzie produced, with appropriate gravity, at eleven thirty on the morning in question in the drawing-room of Wilcot Grange.

"I understand, Miss Delafield, that you have been Mr Frayne's secretary for, let me see now, about two and a half years?" He spoke in the kind of dry pedantic voice which Rose had come to associate with lawyers.

"Yes." Had this man any idea, she wondered, of the real situation? Did he really think that she was just a secretary? He seemed so old, so out of touch. Yet he was obviously finding his task embarrassing. That must mean he had already sensed she was Harvey's mistress and, as such, not a woman with whom he wished to waste much time.

"Did Mr Frayne ever speak to you about his will, Miss Delafield?" he continued.

She thought back. "Yes, once. The subject came up soon after my aunt died when we were discussing her own will."

"And when would that have been?"

She frowned. What possible reason was there for asking such a question? "Last year. Last summer," she answered.

"When he would have told you that he had left half his estate in the form of various trusts to his wife and child, and half in trust to you."

"Yes."

"You realise that your share would have come to a considerable amount. Mr Frayne was a very rich man."

"I . . . did not think about it very much."

"No? Perhaps that is as well. Miss Delafield, I fear I have to tell you that Mr Frayne altered his will only last Thursday, the day before he died. Apart from some generous bequests to members of his staff, the whole of his residual estate now goes to his daughter, his wife having a life interest."

"Oh." She did not know what else to say. The implication of Ernest MacKenzie's words had yet to sink in.

"It will mean, of course, your leaving here. But I have no wish to hurry you. I do not want to cause unnecessary

hardship or distress, especially after such a sad occurrence. In
any case, you would have to remain at Wilcot until after the
inquest."

"*Inquest?*"

He seemed surprised at her own surprise.

"Why yes, Miss Delafield. Has no one warned you? There
will naturally have to be an inquest. Mr Frayne died under
. . . well . . . unusual circumstances. In cases like this the
cause of death has to be established, if possible. As I believe
you were the last to see Mr Frayne alive, your evidence would
be vital."

She could feel her heart pounding. Dear God. She would
have to tell about Stephen. About Harvey's jealousy. It would
all come out. People would know for certain—however much
they had long suspected—what sort of woman she was. All the
servants. Even the housemaid who brought up her early
morning tea, who had a bottom drawer and was saving up to
get married. Ellen was a good girl. Soon she would have a
wedding ring. She, Rose Delafield, was not a good girl and she
did not have a wedding ring. All she had was drawer upon
drawer of the kind of garments which poor Ellen could only
dream about. Rose felt she would rather die than have Ellen
come to the inquest. Involuntarily, she put up her hands and
covered her face.

Her action seemed to affect Mr MacKenzie. His manner
softened. "Please Miss Delafield. Don't distress yourself
unduly. I am sure you will find the coroner very kind, very
courteous, especially under such tragic circumstances." He
coughed, and then went on, "Returning to practicalities,
should you have presents that Mr Frayne has given you from
time to time, you will, of course, be quite at liberty to keep
them. I remember him once mentioning to me that you have a
portrait of yourself which is of outstanding merit."

"Oh, yes. But . . . I have nowhere to go, nowhere to hang
it." She looked at him, bewildered as a child. Her words were
not said in any self-pitying way, merely as a simple statement
of fact.

For the first time Ernest MacKenzie came up against the
full realisation of what his former client had done. This young

woman in front of him was the victim of a savage retaliation, of dead hands stretching out from the grave. He had never found Harvey Frayne an easy man, although he had respected his business acumen.

"You have family, Miss Delafield?" he hazarded.

She shook her head. "I was an only child. My parents are both dead. An aunt took care of me to a certain extent but she is the one I mentioned, who died last year."

"Friends, perhaps. . .?" he enquired again, tentatively, already fearing the same kind of negative reply.

"I . . . seem to have lost touch with those I made at school. I know some artist friends of Mr Frayne's. The husband painted my portrait. But he is in very poor health."

They seemed to have reached an impasse. "I will give the matter some thought," Ernest MacKenzie said slowly. "As I mentioned before, I have no wish to cause you any undue hardship." In the back of his mind, he wondered whether Mrs Thora Frayne and her daughter might be appealed to, although he doubted there would be any favourable response. In the brief dealings he had had with them, neither lady struck him as having much compassion. They would hardly be likely to care about the future of a young woman who, although he found it distasteful to acknowledge the fact, had obviously been wife in all but name to Harvey Frayne. Falling back on the only strategy which came to him at the moment, he changed the subject.

"I believe it has been arranged that I should see the rest of the staff at some point?" He wished he had not said "rest of the staff", thereby implying that she, too, was merely an employee. But fortunately the insinuation seemed to escape her.

"Oh, yes." She looked at her watch. "After lunch." And then, as if suddenly remembering her role as hostess, she jumped up. "Perhaps you would like a glass of sherry. If you'll excuse me a moment, I'll get the butler to bring some in."

She found Robson hovering in the back hall, decanter and glasses on a silver tray beside him. It was obvious that he had been tactfully waiting there, not wishing to disturb them. Knowing that Ernest MacKenzie could now be left in

Robson's capable hands, she went on up to the tower and sat on her bed, wondering whether she could send word that she was not feeling well. To her credit, she managed to join Ernest MacKenzie in the dining-room, but it was a difficult meal for both to get through. She was acutely conscious that she was being waited on by a man who would soon be hearing of a "generous" legacy in gratitude for services rendered, while she, to put it bluntly, was an outsider, a person who had no business to be there, "out on her ear" as Aunt Jackson might have put it. Would the staff know that? Would Mr MacKenzie only read out bits of the will relevant to individuals? But anyone had a right to see a will, hadn't they? She had a vague recollection of her father once offering to go to Somerset House to look one up on behalf of a certain anxious parishioner. But no one at Wilcot would do that, surely. London was too far away. As far as Rose knew, few of the local inhabitants had ever visited the metropolis. On the other hand, they would go to the inquest, wouldn't they? That is, if. . .

"Mr MacKenzie," she asked, when at last coffee had been served and they were once more alone, "can any member of the public attend an inquest?"

He put down his cup. He would have to tell her. But in all his dealings with the law, he had never felt so sorry for anyone in his life.

"Yes, Miss Delafield," he replied. "An inquest is invariably open to the public."

12

The court-room, as Rose had anticipated, was packed on the day of the inquest which, unfortunately, coincided with market-day in Fordingham. She walked hesitantly to the witness box, a thin pale defenceless-looking figure, suitably dressed in black, sadly aware that all eyes were upon her and that the atmosphere was tense, even hostile. To make matters worse, on arrival she had overheard a member of the crowd utter words that she knew she would never forget. They danced about in her brain as she prepared to take the oath: "There goes Mr Frayne's fancy woman," a female voice had said, in a strong west country accent.

Because of the nervous state she had been in since Harvey's death, Mrs Robson had insisted on asking the local G.P. to call. Having hitherto enjoyed good health, Rose had never had occasion to see Dr Fison before. Now, she was grateful for his support. He was a youngish man who had kindly offered to see her through her present ordeal, but today he was naturally unable to help answer the stream of questions which began coming at her in quick succession, as the coroner—a Dr Gorringe—tried to elicit exactly what had happened on the night Harvey had died.

"You say Mr Frayne was upset, Miss Delafield? Not his usual self?"

"Yes."

"Can you tell me what was causing this?"

"I . . . he . . ." She passed a hand over her forehead and then gripped the brass rail surrounding the witness box again. "He . . . was upset with me," she managed to bring out, at last.

"And why was that, Miss Delafield?"

"I . . . he . . ." she repeated, and then stopped.

Dr Gorringe became a little less abrupt. "I am sorry to have to ask you questions of such a personal nature, Miss Delafield, but I am sure you will appreciate that it is necessary to establish just how and why Mr Frayne came to meet his death. I am wondering whether, perhaps, you would prefer to give your evidence sitting down?"

"Thank you." She sank, with relief, on to the seat provided and took a sip of water which had earlier been placed before her.

"You were about to tell me, Miss Delafield," Dr Gorringe continued, after a brief interval, "why Mr Frayne was evidently very distressed that night and why you felt it had something to do with you."

"He thought," she replied, in little more than a whisper, "that I had been . . ." She paused, unable to bring out the word 'unfaithful'. "Disloyal," she said.

"I see."

A murmur went round the court-room. Dr Gorringe quelled it with a quick lift of his hand.

"And had you been, as you put it, disloyal to Mr Frayne?"

"No."

"Did you not therefore disabuse his mind about this misconception?"

"I . . . he didn't give me a chance. He simply left the room."

"Was this a subject which had come up between you before?"

"Yes. Once."

"But not quite so seriously?"

She hesitated. "No," she answered. Although he had hit her then, hadn't he, *and* called her 'whore'.

"Miss Delafield, did Mr Frayne ever say anything to you about taking his own life?"

"Oh, no."

"And after he left you that night, what did you do?"

"I can't remember. I must have gone to bed."

"You never saw him again?"

"No."

"Nor heard him leave the house?"

"No."

"So that the first time you were aware that something was wrong was the following morning when Mrs Robson told you his bed had not been slept in?"

"Yes."

"Miss Delafield, once again, I fear I have to ask you this. Although you say that you have never been disloyal to Mr Frayne, have you, by your conduct, ever given him reason to think you might have been?"

There was sudden and complete silence in the court-room. She reached out to take another sip of water and the sound made by such a small action seemed like an explosion.

"Possibly," she mumbled.

"Were you, perhaps, thinking of leaving Mr Frayne?"

"Oh, no. Nothing like that."

"How long had Mr Frayne been troubled about the situation?"

"Since . . . before Christmas."

"And he questioned you about it then?"

"Yes. That was the time I mentioned, only . . ." The last word slipped out. She could have bitten it back. Dr Gorringe was quick to take her up on it.

"Only what, Miss Delafield?"

She took a deep breath. There was no going back now. "Mr Frayne became very suspicious of my movements after that. I realised I was being watched."

The court-room fairly hummed now. Dr Gorringe was forced to call sharply for silence.

"Yet you maintain that there were no grounds for these suspicions or for such steps to be taken?"

"No. Mr Frayne simply jumped to some wrong conclusions after receiving certain information."

"And these conclusions resulted in him making false accusations against you on the night he died?"

"Yes."

"You must have found the whole situation very painful, Miss Delafield."

"Yes."

"Thank you. I think that will be all for now."

She wished he had not added "for now". What else could he possibly want to know? The identity, possibly, of the man Harvey was jealous of? She was relieved that, at least,

Stephen's name had not been brought into the proceedings.

Mrs Robson and her husband were then called upon in turn. As might have been expected, each gave evidence in exemplary fashion. Robson, who had been last but one to see Mr Frayne before he died, stated that he considered his employer to have been "out of sorts" on the night in question. He had noticed that he had "eaten hardly a morsel" at dinner. Mrs Robson, he said, had been most upset about it, as she had cooked guinea fowl, which Mr Frayne was very "partial to". No, he had not heard any sounds of a quarrel between Miss Delafield and Mr Frayne. They had simply retired to the study and he had locked up, as usual, before going to bed at about ten thirty p.m. He volunteered the information that both Mr Frayne and Miss Delafield were "very quiet people", but that Mr Frayne had been particularly silent that evening. He had omitted to give him his customary greeting on coming into the house after Miss Delafield had driven him down from London, but Robson had put it down to his employer having other things on his mind, probably "a business matter".

Fred Chapman next gave evidence in much the same staid and sober fashion as the Robsons. He related how he had organised a search party consisting of Wilcot's entire outdoor staff, with the addition of Robson, who had been anxious to help; how he had come upon Mr Frayne's body lying "all of a heap like", the shot-gun beside it; how he realised his employer must have been dead some hours; how he had sent for both police and ambulance.

There then followed evidence from the police inspector and the doctor who had examined Harvey's body at the scene of the accident, prior to its removal to Fordingham hospital. Both were in complete agreement that the deceased had died from gun-shot wounds that were almost certainly self-inflicted, sometime shortly before midnight.

To her overwhelming relief, Rose was not called again. There was a quarter of an hour's break while the court adjourned. Then Dr Gorringe returned to deliver his verdict: that the deceased had "committed suicide while the balance of his mind was disturbed".

As Dr Fison took Rose's arm to shepherd her out of the

court-room and down the steps of the Guildhall into his car, her other arm was suddenly taken and a voice said, "My poor sweet. I could hardly bear it for you. The old Hispano is waiting. I'm driving you straight back to London."

She turned, that curiously innocent, vaguely confused look of wonderment on her face. "Oh *Stephen*, how nice. But . . . what about my things? At Wilcot? I must collect my *things*."

"Things, dear Rose," he replied, "are of no importance at a time like this. What is important is that you get to hell out of such a ridiculous, narrow-minded, vindictive neighbourhood immediately."

13

Stephen seemed to think it perfectly natural that Rose should go straight from the home of one man to that of another, without any discussion as to the rights and wrongs of the situation. To him, it was the only thing to do. The question of propriety, reputation or marriage simply did not enter into it. In any case, Stephen did not believe in marriage. Early on in life he had decided that it put paid to romance.

And Stephen was a romantic.

Rose and her strange circumstances had appealed to him from the very beginning. She was a damsel in distress. She was Beauty, Harvey the Beast. He himself was the knight in shining armour. Having tucked her into his car, he let in the clutch and drove away from the precincts of the court-room with a flourish. By the time they were on the A30 to London, he almost had her smiling again.

"You must put it all behind you, darling. It was a ghastly thing to have happened but, well, let's face it, you weren't meant to spend the rest of your life shut up in servitude. Because that's what it amounted to. Harvey must have known what he was doing to you. I expect a lot of the trouble was due to him being consumed by guilt. I wish you'd confided in me more, let me know what was happening these last few months. But never mind. I'll make it up to you. We'll go abroad, the day after tomorrow. Oh damn, I suppose you'll want your things. Perhaps we'd better make it next week. It'll be easy enough to fetch your stuff from Belgravia, including your portrait, but we'll have to persuade that butler's wife to pack up at Wilcot. You *would* like to go abroad, wouldn't you, darling? What about a long leisurely European tour? I know H.S. would love that."

He slowed down, patted the steering-wheel of his beloved Hispano-Suiza fondly, and then dropped the same hand on to her knee, while at the same time giving her a quick glance.

Seeing the expression on her face, he drew in at the nearest gateway, stopped the engine and gathered her in his arms. By the time they reached London, Rose felt that she might have been living with Stephen all her adult life.

She was enchanted by his home. Having only seen it once on the occasion of the rather grand party for which he had apparently hired "flunkeys", as he put it, she soon discovered that his normal way of life was entirely different. The drawing-room in which she had been formally entertained was rarely used, Stephen preferring to spend most of the time in his large extremely untidy study at the back of the house, which led off the kitchen. He said that he cooked many meals himself and she soon discovered he was expert at it. A Mrs Lovewell—"*isn't it a divine name, Rose, such a pet, you'll adore her*"—came all the way from Lambeth each day and stayed from nine until one, seeing to his cleaning, washing, shopping and, if required, would prepare simple dishes. He explained that he had been in the habit of dining out most evenings, although he did not say where or with whom. Rose realised that he must have had plenty of other girl friends, but she was suddenly feeling so happy it seemed better not to enquire.

As it turned out, they did not leave for their holiday until well into June. In his enthusiasm for the idea, Stephen had forgotten that besides being committed to writing several articles for a certain newspaper editor called Guy Thornton, he had also promised him that he would write up the Royal Academy Summer Exhibition. "But perhaps it's just as well, my sweet," he remarked one day, on returning from Fleet Street. "I happened to mention to Guy that I was thinking of doing a European tour, and he got all excited and suggested I might not only do a piece on French chateaux, but he'd like a bit about art in Germany today. This chap Hitler must be a complete moron. By frightening away people like poor Carl, he's left with a country which has sacrificed beauty for the boot. Guy wants me to do some research on this. It seems like a good idea, as long as I don't get thrown into a German clink for it. Besides, it'll bring in a few pennies. Help to pay for our trip, so to speak."

It was the first time Stephen had touched on finance. From

the extravagant way he carried on, Rose had assumed that he had no difficulties in that direction. Now, she was not so sure. He had told her a little about his background: his parents—a retired colonel and his wife living in the Lake District—a married sister out in South Africa, a rich godmother called Mimi, with whom he stayed when in New York. He had had, so it seemed, a fairly conventional upbringing—Stowe, Oxford and then a year's travelling the world with Mimi, during which they had "done" most of the famous beauty spots, an experience which had fostered and encouraged his love of art. Then, quite by chance, through a college friend, he had met Guy Thornton, who had discovered that he had a natural talent for writing about it.

Considering the depression of the late 'twenties and early 'thirties, Stephen considered he had been "damn lucky". "I was insufferable at one stage," he told Rose. "But then I suppose you could say I made good—as well as a bit of bad," he added, with a smile. When she had queried the latter, he had replied, "Well, darling, I still don't lead exactly the kind of life the parents would wish. They'd like me to settle down, supply them with a grandchild. That's why I don't go home very much now. In fact, I'm afraid I've more or less stopped. The trouble was my mother would keep producing what she felt were suitable prospective wives for me: girls who were all pearls and twin-sets and thick ankles. She and my father think I live a rackety life. I daresay I do. But it's such *fun*, especially now it's brought me you."

Stephen made it plain from the start of their relationship that he did not want her to do any typing for him, as it was a task he preferred to undertake himself. He said that he liked to correct as he went along and, as he was invariably up against a deadline, there was never any time to have his manuscripts "tarted up". But since he had referred to the expediency of combining work and pleasure on their forthcoming trip, Rose began wondering whether she ought to say anything to him about financial matters, having come to live with him in such an unpremeditated happy-go-lucky way. Should she explain that, apart from her portrait, her clothes and a little jewellery—Harvey had stuck to his principle of never giving her very much of this for reasons which he had explained early on—she had forty-three pounds, seven shillings and sixpence in her bank account.

So far, she had had few personal expenses and whenever there was a question of household requirements, Stephen had merely tossed some notes at her, rather as he did to Mrs Lovewell, with some lighthearted suggestion such as, "Darling, when you're out, do go and see if that fish shop at the end of the Portobello Road has any more of those gorgeous lobsters." And, dutifully, Rose had gone, managing to make a passable mayonnaise before Stephen returned from personally delivering an article to Fleet Street which should have been there several hours before.

Yet as time went by, Rose sensed that he was very definitely not as affluent as he appeared. She had always known that he was in a completely different class from Harvey when it came to money, but the very casualness with which he treated it probably meant that a lot slipped through his fingers. She realised that she herself was no paragon either when it came to spending the stuff but, until now having been the mistress of an extremely rich man, there had seemed no need to worry. If, as had sometimes been the case, the figures on her bank statement—which Harvey always asked to see—regrettably showed up in red, he instantly arranged for them to be turned into black again. Only once had he made some slight reference to extravagance. It had never occurred to her to think about all the time and effort Harvey put into making his money, nor that he was often under severe strain while so doing. Neither had she given much thought, until now, as to exactly how Stephen obtained his, whether it all came from his writing or whether he was in some way subsidised, probably by Mimi.

When, suddenly, he returned one evening with the most gorgeous Isadora Duncan scarf for her "on the strength" he had said, cheerfully, "of a whopping cheque from Guy", she decided it would perhaps be better to push the subject out of her mind. Stephen was so obviously happy. So was she. Why spoil it? There would be time enough to talk about financial matters, if necessary, when they returned from the continent. Living with him was a never-ending delight. He was so

different from Harvey. There was no banishment to a tower
suite. Although her clothes hung—chiefly because of their
numbers—in one of his spare rooms, she and Stephen
spent all and every night in his enormous double bed, not even
bothering to separate when they heard Mrs Lovewell's key in
the lock each morning.

"I think she's quite emancipated, darling," Stephen had
said, when she had first queried the situation. "I gather her
husband is dead and her children have fled the nest, but she
has a lodger called Joe. Well, she *calls* him a lodger, if you see
what I mean. I know she approves of you wholeheartedly. I
found her studying your portrait in the drawing-room the
other day and do you know what she said? 'Doesn't do Miss
Delafield justice, Mr Forman. She's prettier than that. I do
believe she gets prettier every day'. Do you think that could
be something to do with me, my sweet?" he had added, giving
Rose a sidelong glance.

She remembered that particular conversation while she was
busy packing on the eve of their departure. Looking in the
mirror, as she held up this and that garment to her figure in an
effort to decide exactly what to take, she could not help
thinking perhaps Mrs Lovewell had been right. She saw a
young woman of twenty-one, definitely more rounded than
she had been a year ago, with a face self-assured yet full of
eager anticipation, pleased with life, pleased with herself. She
could not imagine why she had ever bothered to think about
the precariousness of her position. Money was such a bore.
True, she was aware that her bank balance had dwindled
rather alarmingly the last week or so. She had been unable to
resist buying some slave bangles which she had picked up in
the Caledonian market and a pair of wide Marlene Dietrich
slacks.

She happened to be trying on the latter garment when
Stephen's voice came from the doorway. "Charming, my
sweet. Which reminds me. Do you want some cash for this
kind of thing? Most remiss of me not to have asked before."

14

Stephen's idea of a long and leisurely European tour proved far more correct than even he had at first envisaged, especially from the length point of view. For one thing, they started by spending over a month in the Loire valley, at the end of which they were still loath to leave it.

A few miles south of Angers, they found a small wayside inn run by a Monsieur and Madame Hervouët. Here, the friendly atmosphere, coupled with the beauty of the surrounding countryside, had a curiously calming, almost hypnotic, effect on them both. Compared to the luxurious hotel on the Riviera to which Harvey had once taken her, Rose wondered how she could ever have imagined that her life with him had been remotely enjoyable. She became gentler, sweeter, more like the young girl who had grown up in the Norfolk rectory, before so unexpectedly embarking on such an unconventional life. Cut off from the world as she and Stephen now were, the fact that she was, for the second time, living in sin, mattered not at all. Any lingering sense of shame disappeared. She felt she was totally in love with Stephen and he with her. They lived in enchantment, the days and nights merging into each other, so that all sense of time was lost.

When, at the end of July, he murmured something about moving on, it seemed to Rose as if a spell was about to be broken—and she said as much to him.

"Oh, I know, my sweet. I feel that, too. But . . . well, I heard from Guy today. He's delighted with what I've sent him so far, but he did add a tactful reminder about Germany still being on the agenda. He was wondering, if I could possibly manage it, whether I could take in more of Italy en route. Then do some kind of comparison between the two countries under their respective dictators. I have a feeling he'd like a definitely political flavour in whatever I send him. I must say I'd like to have a shot at it. So I'm afraid we'll have to start

pointing H.S. vaguely in the direction of Genoa and then push
on to Florence and Siena. It'll be damned hot at this time of
the year. I hadn't bargained on going quite so far south."

She found he was all too right about the heat. In Florence,
she became ill and had to remain in the hotel for a week,
leaving Stephen to wander off by himself. Once, when it was
well after the hour at which he had said he would be back, she
became panicky. Feeling weak and not being able to speak a
word of Italian, she began to hate the place. Nor, had she been
well, did she think she would have wanted to spend so much
time, as Stephen was doing each day, visiting not only old and
modern art galleries but also universities. She realised that her
own education left much to be desired, but this did not make
her avid for more. She was prepared to listen to whatever
Stephen said on various subjects, but not because of the
knowledge he imparted—simply because he was such an
amusing and cheerful companion. Just being near him was all
that mattered. Ruins, architecture, sculpture, old masters,
surrealism, expressionists, all left her unimpressed. She was
too much a creature of the moment: capricious, sensuous,
despite her deceptive aura of innocence. The only thing she
wanted to do was to love and be loved—and this she had had
in abundance during the past few months.

All at once, she began to resent what she felt to be Stephen's
other love, although she was astute enough to realise that,
however irresponsible he sometimes appeared, his work was
important to him and that he was particularly keen on his
present assignment. He would come back of an evening, drink
a small campari and then, to avoid disturbing her unduly, take
his portable typewriter into their bathroom where, stripped
naked, he would start tapping out some article.

It was not, however, until they reached Germany at the
beginning of September that she began finding his behaviour
not only irksome but also bewildering. A week after they
arrived in Munich, one evening when they were dining in the
open air outside a certain café, he suddenly dropped his voice
and said, "I have a nasty feeling, my darling, that we may be
being followed."

"Followed?" She stared at him. She knew all about being

followed herself, but that anyone should want to do that to them in Germany seemed incomprehensible.

"Don't look round just now. But there's a youngish blond-haired chap behind you about three tables away. I've seen him too often the last few days for it to be a coincidence. After all, we're English, aren't we? I thought they took a hell of a time studying our passports when we crossed the border. I'm glad mine simply had "writer" on it and not "journalist".

She was horrified, as well as scared. "But we haven't done anything wrong, have we? What do they want?"

"To find out what I'm up to and get hold of anything I've written, I guess. Especially anything adverse about the Nazi régime."

"But surely you haven't written anything adverse about it? I thought you said you could understand why Hitler had condemned some of the present-day art as 'degenerate'. And you seemed so impressed the other morning when we saw all those boys and girls marching and dancing in that summer camp by the lake. You remarked on how happy and healthy they looked and what a lot Hitler had done for the youth of the country. How he had given a growing generation new hope."

"Yes, I know." He dropped his voice still further. "But there's another side, Rose. The side the government doesn't want visitors to see, particularly a visiting British journalist. By an odd coincidence, I bumped into a friend from Oxford, Oliver Rudge, the other week. We had a beer together. He's been living out here working on some novel. Being fiction, so far he's got away with it. But it was after our meeting that I sensed I was being trailed. I didn't mention it to you before because I didn't want to alarm you, but now I think it would be as well if we stuck together. I'd sooner you never went out without me."

His words proved uncannily correct. On entering their hotel bedroom that night, they found it had been discreetly searched. It was obvious someone had gone through Stephen's briefcase. All the pieces he had written in Italy were missing.

"Shall you complain to the management?" she asked.

He shook his head. "No, I think not. Better lie low. Fortunately, I can remember most of what I wrote. I certainly shan't put anything on to paper here. I would like to have had one more meeting with Oliver, but it mightn't be wise. Probably the best thing we can do is to head for home."

There was pandemonium at Calais docks when they arrived there on the twelfth of September and the preceding drive had been a nightmare, all like-minded fellow tourists having the same idea: to get out of a country which seemed bent on aggression at all costs, even war.

Back in London, Stephen was never far from the wireless set, listening to reports about Neville Chamberlain, for the first time in his life, boarding an aeroplane and going off to meet Hitler, first at Berchtesgaden, then Godesberg, and finally Munich, in an effort to prevent any invasion of Czechoslovakia.

When, on the last day of the month, the Prime Minister returned to England, waving a piece of paper proclaiming "Peace with Honour", while German troops began pouring into the Sudetenland, Stephen, unaccountably as far as Rose was concerned, let out a stream of savage epithets.

She was completely at a loss. The fact that there was to be no war seemed to her a case for rejoicing, in keeping with the majority of other English people who were said to be swarming into the Mall and along Whitehall, climbing up lamp-posts, singing and crying with relief. Chamberlain was being hailed as a "saviour", the "reincarnation of St George".

"Some reincarnation," said Stephen, bitterly, as he sat behind his typewriter. "We may have got peace, although I doubt it's for long, and there's certainly no honour attached to it. We let the Czechs down, Rose. You can't get away from that. I feel . . . well, ashamed, the same as I did in 1933 when my old college passed a resolution that 'This house will not fight for King and country'. I suppose it's something to do with having a military father, even though I don't see much of him. Maybe I ought to go up to the Lakes next week for a few days."

She became apprehensive. She felt him to be slipping away from her. She realised that it would be impossible for him to take her on a visit to his parents.

"Would you," she asked, diffidently, "join up if there *was* a war?"

"Of course. At once. What do you take me for? A conscientious objector?"

It was difficult to think clearly. She could only ever go by instinct. And that instinct told her that their 'honeymoon' was over.

15

The recruiting officer in the depot at Chiswick was a pale sandy-haired woman with a reserved and vaguely disapproving manner. She reminded Rose of her mathematics mistress at school, for whom she had never been able to do anything right. The room in which they were sitting seemed stifling, a fierce midday sun beating down through the skylight overhead. It was Wednesday, September 6th, 1939—the war with Germany exactly three days old.

It had been a difficult twelve months for Rose, the international situation exacerbating her own personal dilemma. In March, the whole of Czechoslovakia had come under German domination and Carl Scholte, who had been distraught at the time of Munich, now suffered a fatal stroke. Elena was not only grief-stricken but consumed by anger, an anger which was also reflected in Stephen's own behaviour. He was constantly raging against Hitler, the Nazis, Neville Chamberlain, the British government and the way the whole British nation had kept turning a blind eye to what was happening on the continent. He particularly disliked the use of the word "appeasement", which he called merely a euphemism for cowardice.

That summer he had joined the territorials. In August he was called up.

Although on their return from Munich the previous September, Rose had continued to live with Stephen and had never felt the slightest necessity for doing anything else, she became more and more aware as the year progressed that she had been right in assuming their honeymoon period was over. Stephen, when not actually writing or voicing his opinion, was sometimes so preoccupied that she wondered if he had forgotten her existence. He spent a great deal of time with Guy Thornton, who frequently came straight from his office in Fleet Street to dine with them. Not being their intellectual equal and unable to contribute to the conversation, she would retire as soon as the meal was over, scarcely conscious of Stephen getting into bed beside her during the early hours of the morning.

On the evening before he left for an officers' training camp at Catterick, he did, however, have a long talk to her. She was surprised, even touched, by his solicitude.

"Look, Rose. It's coming now. This war. There's no getting away from it. I'm worried about leaving you. I mean, what'll you do?" He became all at once diffident, slightly embarrassed. "You see, by an odd coincidence, the lease of this place expires soon. I would have mentioned it before, but I didn't want to worry you. A month ago I was on the point of asking the landlords if they would renew it. Then, when it became so obvious what was going to happen, I felt it mightn't be such a good idea. They don't allow sub-lets. I hardly imagine you'd fancy staying here alone, would you? And London might not be the most healthy spot to be in if they start bombing. I was thinking . . . well, you'll probably want to do some kind of war work, I expect."

She hadn't thought. She was not like him over such issues. She had been banking on Mr Chamberlain pulling off another hat-trick, of Stephen remaining a part-time soldier, going off to do his evening square-bashing twice a week on some parade ground near Blackheath. Patriotism, feeling for the oppressed, social conscience—even though she *had* been a rector's daughter—seemed nowadays to pass her by. Because Stephen had been doing so well with his writing—more and more articles of a purely political nature kept appearing in the press—she had conveniently been able to forget her one-time concern as to whether she could or should contribute to the household expenses. She had allowed herself to be lulled into a false sense of security, relying on the one thing she knew something about: love, particularly the physical aspect. That her present lover was actually suggesting that she should look to wider horizons, become more responsible for herself, came as something of a shock.

When she did not answer at once, he went on, "Darling, don't get me wrong. But I'll only have periodic leave. We could still spend some of it together. I mean, if you joined one of the women's organisations, I believe they're quite sympathetic about that sort of thing. Unless, of course, I get sent abroad."

"*Abroad?*" She was scared, more for herself, perhaps, than for him.

"Yes. God knows what'll happen when the balloon goes up, but one thing's certain. If we're going to beat Hitler, we'll all have to do our bit."

That was why, on a scorching September day, Rose found herself sitting before this spinsterish, matter-of-fact-looking female, who was now asking for her qualifications.

"I can type," she answered, somewhat defensively.

"Ah." The pen of her interrogator flew quickly over the form on the makeshift desk.

"And drive," Rose added, as an afterthought.

"*Drive?*"

"Yes."

There was a pause. The recruiting officer frowned. "There are quite a few young women clamouring to join the F.A.N.Ys just now, I believe. But the country is more in need of those with secretarial qualifications. I suggest you apply for a clerical post. Perhaps you would sign here."

Rose had signed, hoping she was doing the right thing. Having done so, she could not help thinking that she was once again shifting the responsibility for herself—not this time on to some man, but on to the Women's Auxiliary Territorial Service, who would do as it wished with her.

During the few weeks before she was actually called up, she managed to arrange for all Stephen's furniture to be put into store and placed her own possessions—including her portrait—in the care of Elena, who seemed only too delighted to have what she called "Carl's masterpiece" under her roof.

By the middle of October, Private Rose Delafield, hair shortened and kitted out in khaki, found herself sleeping with eleven other members of the A.T.S. in a hut in the grounds of a large manorial house near Oxford.

Rose did not know what to make of her room-mates. On her left there was a young cockney called Rita Maltby; on her right a taciturn middle-aged woman by the name of Elizabeth Renton, who said little other than good morning and good night. At the far end of the hut there was a large extrovert type, who Rose suspected might fit in to Stephen's "pearls-and-twin-set" brigade. But although she at first tried to single Rose out as a companion, it soon became evident that Diana Fleming had changed her mind. Sadly, Rose realised that she was regarded as an unknown quantity, a misfit. She was a woman who had been a mistress twice over—not that anyone in Hut C was to know that. But she knew that they sensed there was something suspect about her. For all the occasional lewd talk at night, she was sure she was the only one among them who was not a virgin. The knowledge made her uneasy. She became withdrawn, going about her daily duties of cleaning, helping in the cook-house, attending lectures and being drilled, with increasing distaste. She wished she had not listened to the advice of the recruiting officer and had joined the F.A.N.Ys. Driving a car, driving *officers*, would have been so much more glamorous. In short, she had been a fool.

Each day she looked for a letter from Stephen, but when one at last arrived it was disappointingly short. He said that he was enjoying the course as a means to an end, but was hardly given a moment to himself. He hoped that she was not being treated quite so rigorously. He ended by saying that he missed her and loved her, but there was no mention of possible leave or their meeting.

During the second week at the A.T.S. base, all the new recruits were subjected to inoculations against typhoid and tetanus. Afterwards, there was much distress, even wailing, in the hut. Most of the occupants, having never been away from home before, kept calling out for their mothers, saying they had never felt so ill. In fact, health—or rather, ill-health—seemed to figure a good deal in the general conversation, especially amongst the townee element, who found the imposition of flat lace-up shoes a real physical hardship, their aching previously unused muscles having to get used to a completely new stance. Rose, who had been accustomed to wearing both types of footwear, was amongst the very few who were unaffected by such problems.

Yet she had plenty of others, mostly of a psychological kind. At the beginning of November, she found herself posted to a company of A.T.S. serving Southern Command Headquarters and billeted in a house called Hemmings, not far from Wilcot Grange. She was unable to get away from the feeling of having made a complete come-down. Less than two years ago she had been, to all intents and purposes, lady of the manor, even if she had not possessed a wedding ring. She had been waited on, worn Hartnell and Molyneux clothes and had her portrait hung in the R.A. She might not have had quite so much material luxury after taking up with Stephen, but nevertheless their life together had been rich and exciting in an entirely different way. Now, she was reduced to wearing khaki issue, made to salute her superiors—both men and women—and ordered to report at eight thirty each morning to a central registry in a vast stately home, having already made her bed and queued for breakfast. To add insult to injury, she had not yet been asked to use her secretarial experience which the recruiting officer had seemed so keen on—only to spend long and wearisome hours like some post office clerk, simply sorting army communications and carefully placing them into labelled boxes, to be subsequently whisked away at certain intervals by various A.T.S. personnel acting as messengers. It was like being in a treadmill, names such as G.Ops, Staff Duties, R.S.M. or Catering still dancing before her eyes, as she tried, unsuccessfully, to go to sleep after lights out back in the cramped bedroom she shared with three others in a house which the army had commandeered.

Occasionally, a crash-helmeted despatch rider would appear at the registry with a special missive marked URGENT, TOP SECRET, for which she would have to sign. Then, asking him to wait and getting a girl at a neighbouring desk to stand in for her for a few minutes, she would hurry up the long stone staircase from the cloisters and knock on the appropriate door.

Whenever one such message was for the G.Ops room, she often encountered a certain Major Somerville, who seemed to keep her longer than any of the other officers before signing the second receipt for which she was obliged to ask.

Eventually, he would hand it to her, while at the same time giving her a slightly amused appraising look before she took her leave. She did not really mind. It was a look she had come to know. She had seen it on the faces of quite a few men lately, officers and other ranks alike. She had managed to make certain alterations to her uniform—much as she loathed it—so that it fitted rather well and it was good to feel that she was still attractive to the opposite sex, in spite of the khaki issue she was forced to wear, day in and day out. It began to dawn on her that she could, if she wished, find a little diversion from her present monotonous existence.

She began to welcome the opportunities to visit the G.Ops room in the hopes of seeing Major Somerville.

16

She was asked out by Henry Somerville at the beginning of December. After signing for a secret document she had brought him, he said, quite casually, "If you're not doing anything tomorrow evening, I wonder if you'd care to meet me at Ford's garage where my car is being serviced? I thought we might go and have a meal somewhere."

"I . . . yes, thank you very much. I should love to." She found herself blushing in rather the same way as she had in previous similar situations.

"Good. I believe you don't get off until six. Say six-fifteen, then? You know where Ford's is, I expect. At the end of Bell Lane. Incidentally . . ." he paused and then continued, "it might be as well not to say too much about it to anyone."

"Yes. I understand."

She went back to the registry, not only feeling cheered but strangely excited. She knew perfectly well what Major Somerville was getting at. Fraternisation between officers and other rank A.T.S. was frowned upon—in public. But there was no denying that it did take place clandestinely. At official entertainments the two strata of the forces were strictly segregated. They did not attend each other's dances, for instance, nor were they seen in each other's company during the day unless it was on some specific duty, such as those somewhat privileged girls who worked for the camouflage officer and sometimes got taken out to make sketches of the countryside, from which they could subsequently produce models. One corporal in charge of that department had actually been taken up in an old biplane by Major Massing-ham to see what the lie of the land looked like from the air, causing considerable envy amongst her contemporaries.

Rose was aware that she, too, would be a target for jealousy, gossip and probably overt disapproval if she were to reveal her prospective assignation. She therefore went about her preparations quietly, simply applying for a late pass, washing her hair and making sure that she had a pair of good new stockings, however much she wished they could have been flesh silk instead of drab lisle regulation ones.

Henry Somerville was waiting for her when she walked down Bell Lane a little after six fifteen the following night. In the light of a fitful moon she saw him get out of his car and go round to the passenger door, which he held open for her. He then drove off quickly past the blacked-out houses, saying little until they were well into the open countryside.

"I thought we might go to a roadhouse not far from Fordingham, which produces quite a passable meal."

"*Fordingham?*"

"Do you know the town then?" Her violent reaction had obviously startled him.

She hesitated a moment, trying to recover her equilibrium. "Yes, I do. But it's rather further than I was expecting."

"Not more than fifteen miles, if one uses the back roads. And I've got the petrol. You're not worried about time, are you? I mean, I imagined you'd make some kind of special arrangement."

"Oh, yes. I have a late pass. Until midnight."

He turned and gave her a puzzled look. "There's nothing *wrong* with Fordingham then, is there?"

"Oh no. It just happens that I was living in the area some time ago." She regretted her words as soon as she had uttered them.

"Really? Where, exactly?"

"Nowhere you'd know. A small village called Wilcot."

It was his turn now for unexpected revelations.

"As matter of fact, I know it very well. You see, I share a cottage with the camouflage expert, Edward Massingham, on a nearby estate. We rent it from the owner, Sir Reginald Farquharson. I think it was occupied by one of his unmarried employees who got called up, so the place was empty. It's pretty primitive, but neither of us relished the thought of living in some official billet, especially Edward, being an artist. If you like, we might call in there on the way back. Incidentally, do call me Henry. You're Rose, aren't you?"

"Yes."

She felt she wanted time to digest all his information and was grateful when he did not press further questions on her during dinner. Yet she sensed he was only playing a waiting game. His was a disturbing presence. He was a dark, powerfully-built man, whose curious eyes appeared to be constantly sizing her up in a lazy sensual way. Although he behaved with the utmost courtesy throughout their meal, in which he related some amusing anecdotes connected with his background, when they got up to go she felt that he was well aware that a question-mark hung over her own, that she was not a virgin and, what was more, she knew that he knew. There seemed an indefinable mutual understanding between them, as he helped her into the car again and wrapped a rug protectively round her legs.

When they arrived at Larcombe cottage, she was not altogether surprised to find it in darkness, nor when he remarked, on entering, "I suppose Edward's stopping the night in London. He had an interview with some brass hats at the War Office today and told me if he wasn't back by nine, he would put up at his club."

She was acutely conscious that it had just gone nine when they left the roadhouse and that she was not due back at Hemmings until twelve. She watched in fascination as Henry Somerville went across the room, put a match to the laid fire in the grate and pushed a sofa as near to it as possible.

"It's bloody cold here, I'm afraid, but it'll get warmer in a minute, I hope. How about a little brandy to speed up the process?"

"Thank you."

After he had poured out two glasses, he came and sat beside her. "Tell me," he said, suddenly coming straight to the point. "Did something go wrong for you at Wilcot?"

"I suppose . . . yes, you could say that." She thought: what exactly did go wrong? Perhaps it was not so much *what* went wrong as that *I* went wrong. Because that's what everyone calls it. Going wrong. Living in sin. Taking the downward path. But was I so very wicked? I can't help it if I happen to like something that's so very pleasurable, can I? And the circumstances were exceptional. I suppose if I hadn't been initiated into such pleasures early on, I might be different now. But I was and I'm not. It's three months since I slept with Stephen. And he doesn't write much. In his last letter he said something about going home when he got leave because his mother wasn't well. Does he expect me not to mind? Not to miss him? Not to miss what went on between us?

"You were saying . . .?" Henry Somerville prompted her, "about what went wrong."

She cupped the glass—albeit a cheap one— of brandy in her hands, rather as Harvey Frayne had taught her. "I was living at Wilcot Grange," she replied, slowly, "when there was a . . . tragedy."

"You mean the owner's suicide? I've heard a bit about that from the people who live there now, the Fishers. Edward and I sometimes get asked over there. I'm sorry. I hope he was no relation of yours?"

"No. He was no actual . . . relation."

She wished she had not put in the word 'actual'. She felt his eyes upon her, even though she remained staring at her glass.

"I see." He got up and threw another log on the fire. Then he sat back and took her hand. "Poor Rose," he said.

Except for an occasional splutter from the hearth, there was silence in the room. She recalled other evenings which she had spent not far away, strange and unnatural ones, while Harvey read and she pretended to until she would stand up and say, "I think I'll go to bed now." She remembered his brief nod and how she would take herself up to the tower suite where she would wait, often trembling, as she listened for his footsteps on the stairs.

Thank God there was nothing like that about the present atmosphere. It was infinitely comforting having Henry Somerville holding her hand. It seemed even more comforting when he slipped his whole arm round her waist.

"Poor Rose," he repeated, as she lifted her face to be kissed.

17

In the spring of the following year, several things happened more or less at once. Henry Somerville was suddenly posted at less than twenty-four hours' notice. Rose was transferred to an entirely different branch of the Command, where she found herself crammed into a Nissen hut, working in a round-the-clock typing pool along with twenty others. And, as she was queuing for her weekly pay of eleven shillings one Friday, she noticed, ahead of her, the back view of someone wearing a lance-corporal's stripe on her arm, who seemed vaguely familiar. When the girl in question went up to the desk, smartly saluted the C.O., collected her pay packet and returned down the line towards Rose, she realised, with a shock, who it was.

"Susan!"

"Miss Delafield!"

The greeting was spontaneous, Susan automatically lapsing into her one-time mode of address. Heads turned, quickly followed by a peremptory call for order by the sergeant in charge of the parade. Susan walked on, but Rose had little doubt that she would be waiting for her outside the company office, a supposition which proved entirely correct.

"I could hardly *believe* it," the younger girl said, as they met up. She seemed quite beside herself with pleasure and excitement, as she continued, quickly, "Let's go to the NAAFI. Where are you billeted? Have you been here long? Where do you work? What a *marvellous* piece of luck being posted to the same place." It was all Rose could do to keep up with her enthusiasm and spate of questions.

At last, when they had procured two cups of coffee—for which Rose insisted on paying—and were seated, she managed to ask, "But what about you, Susan? And do please remember I'm Rose, not Miss Delafield or, rather, Private Delafield. I see you're a lance-corporal. Congratulations."

Susan Buckley made a grimace. "Oh, *that*. Heaven knows why I got singled out. I'm seconded to the camouflage unit, incidentally. But as a matter of fact I sometimes feel guilty about being in the A.T.S. at all. You see, I started working for Daddy on the farm when war broke out. I could drive a tractor and it seemed the sensible thing to do, because his foreman was a reservist and got called up. But then, being a key agricultural worker, he was suddenly released and came back. So just before Christmas I thought I'd like to get myself into uniform. You know, not just stay at home being a glorified land-girl, where I didn't feel I was doing a proper job. I nearly joined the F.A.N.Y.s, but Mummy vetoed that idea because my night sight has never been too good and she kept worrying about all the dimmed headlights. So I signed on as an AT. I was sent to Eastern Command after my initial training. Then, last February poor Daddy had a heart attack, so I applied for a compassionate posting. He's much better now, thank goodness, but I often wonder if I shouldn't have stayed at home. It would have been nice for Mummy. Look, you simply *must* come and see them both. When's your next day off?"

"I'm not . . . sure."

"But we must synchronize somehow. There's a bus from here to Fordingham which goes all round the villages. It'll be such fun. My parents would adore to see you."

The last thing Rose wanted to do was to visit the Buckleys and she felt quite certain that Anne Buckley, at least, would not want to see her. She had been very aware that Susan's mother had strongly disapproved of her daughter's youthful infatuation and, after what had eventually taken place at Wilcot Grange, she must have been very glad that Rose's departure had been so swift and final. She wondered how much Susan had heard about it. There was bound to have been a lot of talk. Perhaps that was why the girl had suddenly begun to look embarrassed.

"It must have been awful for you," Susan was now saying. "About what happened. I'm so sorry. I wished I could have done something to help. I wanted to write . . . only no one seemed to know where you'd gone. I thought of you no end."

"That was very kind of you, Susan."

"I went to the art college in Fordingham after I left school, you know. I suppose that's why I'm in camouflage now. I wanted to go to London, study at the Slade, but Mummy wouldn't hear of it. She seemed to think something terrible would happen to me." Susan broke off and giggled slightly. "You know, *men*. I honestly think she thought I'd get picked up by the white-slave traffic and she'd never see me again. I suppose that's why I was so keen to get away from home when the war came. It seemed like a means of escape. Oh dear, I shouldn't say that, should I? I mean it's *awful* there being a war, but nothing much has happened yet, has it?"

"No. Not yet."

"Do you like it, though, Rose? In the A.T.S.? I wonder what made you join. Did your family mind? I bet they look forward to getting you back on leave."

"I. . ." She wished the girl would not ask so many questions, that she was not so hopelessly naïve. "I don't have any family, I'm afraid, Susan. On my last leave I went to stay with a friend, the widow of an artist who once painted my portrait. I remember your parents meeting them both when I first came to Wilcot."

"Oh, I'm *terribly* sorry. I didn't realise."

Rose wondered what Susan would have said if she had told her that she had nowhere else to go other than Elena's and that her former boy-friend, Lieutenant Stephen Forman, with whom she had been living, had been sent to France with the British Expeditionary Force. But there was little time for speculation. Susan prattled on again, well-meaning, eager. How old would she be now? Rose guessed she must be about nineteen. She herself was only four years her senior, yet she felt as if it might have been twenty. Susan was so completely unsophisticated, sincere, a young woman utterly without guile. Rose felt that they should have swapped christian names. It was Susan who was the typical English rose.

Across the small table in the crowded NAAFI, the older woman studied her. She was certainly extremely pretty now, but Rose sensed it was a prettiness which was almost too sweet, too fresh, to attract many young men. It was quite possible that Susan had not yet even been kissed. Rose wished fervently that they had never met up again. Something inside her kept saying: I am no good to you. Don't you *understand*?

It was a relief when she heard her say, "The powers that be want me to put in for O.C.T.U. You know, get a commission. I suppose I'll have to. Daddy says one sort of owes it to the nation if one's been given a good education. I'm sure you'll do that, won't you, Rose? You'd make such a super officer."

"Not necessarily."

"But why on earth not? Look how splendidly you took care of. . ." Susan began stumbling over her words a little and then brought out, "Well, things at the Grange."

Rose turned away. There were some soldiers at the next table. She knew they had been discussing them, but that it was she herself in whom they were interested, not Susan. Anger welled up inside her. She felt besmirched.

"Look," she said. "I've got to go now. It's been lovely seeing you, Susan."

The girl's so obvious disappointment at her hurried departure seemed like a reproach.

She walked back to Hemmings through the grounds of the stately home which, but for one small flat, had been given over by its owners entirely to the army. It was mid-April, a wind whipping across the lake, tossing the daffodils hither and thither. She shivered slightly in her khaki uniform, though not from cold. She was more disturbed than she cared to admit. What was she to do now, with Susan Buckley around who would be sure to keep searching her out. Now that the girl was working for Major Massingham, she might even discover that Rose had often been over to Larcombe cottage in the company of his friend, Henry Somerville. She remembered how she had been caught alone there with Henry one day when Diana Fisher had made an unexpected call inviting "whoever was around", as she put it, to drinks that evening. There had been an awkward silence. Rose had given Henry a desperate look and been grateful to hear him say, with great presence of mind, that they were leaving in an hour as they both had duties back at the Command. She knew Diana Fisher was not convinced, but she had taken herself off again with an, "Oh dear. What a bore. Some other time, then."

"That's the devil of not being on the telephone," Henry had said, as he watched her figure, in its immaculate tweed suit, disappearing out of the gate. "Never mind, Rose. Don't be upset. You and I have better things to do with our time here, haven't we?" And he had given one of his low, lazy, teasing laughs, which she always found irresistible.

And now Henry was gone, posted to somewhere on the coast. She wasn't sure how much his departure might have been to do with his private life or whether it was connected with a prevailing growing sense of unease throughout the H.Q. Other ranks were never told much, but she couldn't help sensing that the so-called "phoney" war was possibly coming to an end. The Germans had invaded Denmark and Norway. Finland appeared to have given in. One girl in the typing pool had suddenly been made a lance-corporal and was now engaged on secret work for the G.Ops department. Rose wished it could have been her, even though Henry was no longer there. She got the feeling that she did not rate very highly in the eyes of either her superiors or her contemporaries. She had no great wish for responsibility but she wondered whether she would remain a private for the duration.

If only she had joined the F.A.N.Y.s.

18

She heard the trucks rumbling past Hemmings all night. She knew what they contained: soldiers, soldiers in every degree of exhaustion. It was June. The survivors of the B.E.F. were coming back from Dunkirk.

The alert had gone out in the middle of May. All leave was cancelled. Road blocks began appearing everywhere. There was a continuous stream of despatch riders carrying messages to and fro at the Command. It was rumoured that Fordingham station was like a battlefield, that train-loads of British and French troops were either passing through or being made to alight, from whence they were herded into the vehicles now keeping Rose awake.

Makeshift assembly stations and camps had sprung up like mushrooms in the surrounding countryside. Shops became temporarily cleared of stock. Tea, sugar, bread and margarine were rushed to women volunteers at various service depots, who cut sandwiches hour by hour and then distributed them as required. Three hundred and thirty-eight thousand men needed to be sheltered, fed and re-grouped. The injured had to be hospitalised. As the days and nights passed, Winston Churchill, now Prime Minister, rallied the nation with his most famous speech in the House of Commons: "We shall fight on the beaches, . . . on the landing-grounds, . . . in the fields, . . . in the streets, . . . in the hills. . ., we shall *never* surrender." The whole world looked on with astonishment— and admiration. Great Britain intended to go it *alone*.

Rose wondered what had happened to Stephen, whether he had survived. In odd, unreal moments she imagined she might see him passing by, sitting at the back of some open truck. She knew it was an irrational thought but would she *ever* know how he had fared? She had only received one letter from him since he had left for France. It had arrived on a day when she was meeting Henry. Somehow she had felt guilty about that, even though it was plain that her affair with Stephen was over. He must surely have formed some other attachment by now. She knew he was not a man likely to remain long without female companionship. Nor, she supposed, if the truth be known, was she a woman who could get along easily without a relationship with the opposite sex.

It was rather in this frame of mind that one evening in late July, after she came off duty at the typing pool, she took herself off along the river path at the back of Hemmings which eventually led to Eresby House, an officers' convalescent home. Up until the time of Dunkirk the place had been virtually empty. Now, it was overflowing. If she had been a more self-analytical character, she might have been aware of the subconscious forces which frequently made her gravitate in this direction. But, for the moment, she felt it was simply a love for the river, which reminded her of her Norfolk childhood. Yet at the end of her walk she would often find herself sitting down in the meadows and staring across at the gardens of Eresby House, taking note of the V.A.D.s in their white starched aprons and fetching little butterfly caps, as they darted about the lawns, pushing wheel-chairs, carrying trays or arming some hapless individual towards a deckchair or wooden seat. From the distance, there seemed something curiously attractive about the scene—even *good*—despite the reasons which had brought it about. The nurses looked such veritable angels of mercy. Having constantly regretted not joining the F.A.N.Y.s, Rose felt more sorry than ever that she had not thought of nursing. Surely it would have been more in keeping with her upbringing.

Tonight, as she sat on a small wooden bridge spanning a tributary of the main stream, her khaki uniform seemed more than usually ugly and restrictive. She had a sudden desire to throw caution to the winds, take it off and dive into the pool she had just passed. She recalled the occasions when she and Stephen had swum together on their holiday. Once, when they had not brought their bathing things and happened to be in a particularly secluded spot, they had gone into a river naked. Afterwards, as he began to make love to her, he had gently teased her that she was a young woman ahead of her time. The memory came back now: bright, hurtful and intensely private.

"Hello!" A voice hailed her. She turned to see where it was coming from. Then there was another sound: this time of parting rushes and, suddenly, a tall, painfully thin young man stood before her.

"Mind if I sit down, too?"

"No. Not at all."

"I'm due back at Eresby any minute for nosh. But it seems such a pity to be indoors on an evening like this."

"Yes."

He was fair, practically ash blond. His features were sharp, somewhat patrician, his eyes intensely blue. She judged him to be younger than herself. In manner, he reminded her of Susan.

"You're a patient at Eresby House, then?" she asked, a little uncertain how to deal with so direct an approach.

"Yes. I got a bit of shrapnel in the leg at Dunkirk. Some guy in a hospital near Brighton did a marvellous job getting it out. Then I got sent on here."

"I'm so sorry."

"You needn't be. I'm one of the lucky ones when I think of what happened to some poor devils. I really ought to be getting back to my regiment soon. After a spot of leave, perhaps. Can't think why they're hanging on to me so long here."

"Where is your home?"

"In the north. A little village called Kinton at the foot of the Pennines. My father's the parson there."

"Really? My father was a parson also."

"Was?"

"Yes. He died . . . some time ago, I'm afraid."

It was he who now said, "I'm sorry." After a while, he went on, "What do you do in the A.T.S.?"

"Typing."

"Isn't that rather boring?"

"Yes. Very."

"You might have done better to have joined the Red Cross. I'm sure you'd be jolly good tending the sick at Eresby."

She laughed. He really was extraordinarily like Susan in his enthusiasm and artlessness. "It's too late now, I think. One signs on for the duration."

"I suppose so. But never mind. You'll soon be an officer, won't you?"

"I don't . . . think so."

He regarded her, wide-eyed. "Why on earth not?" It was embarrassing how similar to Susan's was his reaction to her doubtful attitude.

She looked away. She could see a whole bevy of V.A.D.s coming out into the garden of the convalescent home to collect their patients and all their paraphernalia. She evaded her companion's question by saying, "Look, it seems as though you were right about your nosh."

He frowned, rising to his feet awkwardly. She suspected his leg was far from healed. And there was something else about him which disturbed her. During their conversation she had been aware of a pronounced nervous tic affecting one of his eyelids. It was obvious, in more ways than one, that he had by no means got over Dunkirk.

"Will you come here again?" he asked. "Tomorrow. Same time. Or a bit earlier, if you can manage it?"

She sensed that her acquiescence was important to him. It was difficult to refuse. She had never felt that she had personally done very much towards the war effort. Before Dunkirk it had hardly seemed to matter. Now, it was different. Had not Churchill warned the nation some weeks ago that the Battle of Britain was about to begin? And here was this poor young man, already wounded in a previous battle, asking for so little: simply that she would meet him again by the river in twenty-four hours' time. It wasn't going to *hurt* her, for goodness sake, was it? It seemed the least she could do.

"I'll try," she replied.

After she had waved him goodbye and was on her way back to Hemmings, two thoughts came into her mind. One was that she ought to introduce him to Susan. She might even bring the girl along with her next day. The other, following directly from that, was the realisation that she did not even know his name.

He was waiting for her the following evening when she came up the river path slightly earlier than before. She had been unable to contact Susan, who appeared to have gone home for the day. As yet, Rose had managed to avoid accompanying her. It had not been too difficult at first, especially when all leave was cancelled, but lately she had begun to suspect that she might not be able to put it off much longer, unless she could somehow redirect the young girl's adoration of herself into more suitable, healthier channels. To Rose, her new companion and Susan Buckley seemed made for each other.

As soon as she had greeted him, she came straight to the point. "I don't yet know your name."

"Nor me yours. I realised what a fool I'd been as soon as we parted. I thought how on earth could I contact you again if you didn't turn up tonight. I'd have had to ring the G.O.C. and ask him to send out an S.O.S. for the most beautiful AT in England, with auburn hair, gorgeous eyes, creamy complexion, perfect figure, with whom I have fallen head over heels in love."

She was taken completely aback. She also felt afraid. Even Stephen, at his most romantic, had never behaved quite so precipitately. She did her best to pass his remarks off as a joke by saying, "And have me put on a charge, most likely. Please be serious. My name is Rose Delafield. And yours?"

"John St Clair. I knew you'd have a marvellous name, somehow. Rose is perfect. Perfect Rose."

She felt distinctly uncomfortable now. Enough was enough. If he was so susceptible to the opposite sex, why hadn't he fallen for one of the glamorous, graceful figures who had been ministering to him at Eresby House? She would have to put a stop to this. After tonight, she would not meet him again, with or without Susan.

19

The package with the Applethwaite postmark arrived in the middle of August. She turned it over, already knowing and fearing its content. Applethwaite. The Lake District. Stephen's home ground. But it was not Stephen's writing. Her hand shook a little when she summoned up courage to cut the string.

Wrapped around a pile of her own letters was one from his father. "Dear Miss Delafield," it ran,

I must apologise for my seeming tardiness in not getting in touch with you before. But it is only recently that my wife and I have had confirmation of the death of our beloved son. Ever since Dunkirk we have lived in hopes that he might have been taken prisoner. Those hopes, alas, have been finally brought to an end by an official communication from the War Office.

During his last leave, Stephen left a few personal possessions in our care, including the enclosed correspondence from yourself from which I was able to ascertain your address. I have not read the letters, other than to note by their beginning and end that you must have been close to each other.

I wonder if you knew that after the Germans broke through in the Ardennes, Stephen held a bridge practically single-handed, for which he was awarded the M.C.

My wife joins me in sending you every good wish,
   Yours sincerely,
    Geoffrey Forman

She did not cry. She simply sat there on her bed at Hemmings, stunned and anguished. True, their affair had been over. For all she knew, Stephen might have been holding that bridge, winning his M.C., while she had actually been in the arms of another man. She was overcome by guilt—and something more: a feeling of total inadequacy and frustration.

She clenched and unclenched her hands, wanting to lie down and pound them against the bullet-hard mattress. What *was* the war all about? It was so strange. A whole winter without incident. And then this massive German onslaught which had taken the lives of people like Stephen Forman. "Brilliant," she remembered Guy Thornton having once called him. And why, since Hitler had won such an overwhelming victory, had he not sent his armies straight on over across the Channel?

To get up now, as she knew she would have to, and go to the typing pool, took all Rose's courage. At lunchtime, she received another of John St Clair's interminable messages, begging her to meet him "Just once more," as he put it, "to clear up something which has been bothering me. I have waited every evening since we first met. In case you came. I shall do so tonight."

In a kind of desperation, she thought: why not? Anything to get out of this all-female claustrophobic atmosphere at Hemmings—even the name of the house suggests a prison—and find some man, any man, who would, if only for a little while, help me to forget.

She found him walking towards her before she ever reached the little bridge, saw him start to hurry, his whole face lighting up.

"Rose!"

"Hello, John."

"Shall we walk a little?" He pointed. "Over there. Where we shan't be overlooked."

"As you like."

He led her to a group of willows, their base overgrown with bushes: thickthorn, blackberry, elder. But at the bole of one tree there appeared to be a clear space where the grass had been flattened. She wondered if he often came there. Eresby House was quite hidden from view.

They sat down. She leaned back against the tree trunk. John remained more upright, his hands clasped round his knees.

"You said there was something bothering you," she said. "Something you especially wanted to see me about."

"Yes. I felt it was only right. When you seemed to be

avoiding me, I suspected that you must have someone else. Have you?"

"No."

"No?" He turned round and stared at her, with obvious astonishment and relief. "Thank God," he said, and then, after a moment, "You see, if there had been, I would have had to stop pestering you, I suppose. It wouldn't have been cricket. Although I can still hardly believe you have no one."

"Why not?" His reference to cricket made her wince. It was all so typical, coming from him.

"Because you have *everything*. Everything I've ever wanted in a woman."

"But you've only met me twice before. You know nothing about me."

"I know enough." He was kneeling beside her now, almost in supplication.

It was very still in the meadow. In a cornfield on the opposite hill she could see a line of men stooking oats, some of them in khaki trousers, bare to the waist down. She knew that an S.O.S. had gone out to the Command from local farmers for help in getting in the harvest. An aeroplane came into view in the distance, "one of ours", as people said, and then headed in the direction of a nearby aerodrome. Save for the movement of the reapers and the plane, the scene seemed static, caught in the golden evening light, like some beautiful object encapsulated for all time in amber.

She edged herself a little further down on the grass. She thought how easy it would be to seduce him. She had only to put out a hand. Then she rejected the idea yet, almost without being aware of it, she made a gesture which had never failed in her dealings with men. She lowered her eyelids and slightly parted her lips. It was a reflex action, spontaneous, automatic.

He began kissing her, gently at first and then with increasing urgency. She started teasing him a little, pretending to hold back and then giving in. The depression which had engulfed her since receiving Geoffrey Forman's letter and which had made her turn to John St Clair disappeared. A familiar sense of power and excitement took hold of her. Lovemaking was something she knew she could do well, something she understood. During their next long embrace she parted her lips further, pushing her tongue against his.

She was, however, quite unprepared for what happened next. She had never before encountered anything like it. She felt a shudder go through him. Then he sat up abruptly and put his arms round his knees, adopting his previous position. Presently she saw his shoulders heave and realised that he was crying.

"I'm sorry," he said, at last. "I don't know what came over me."

"There is no need to be sorry."

"But don't you *see*? I lost control of myself." He covered his face in his hands. "I didn't mean to let go, to let things get so far."

"Nothing wrong took place."

"But it might have. Supposing . . . well, I could have made you pregnant. I always vowed I'd never . . . well, not until I married." He turned round, the nervous tic affecting his eye more pronounced than she'd ever known it. "Rose, darling. You will, won't you? Marry me, I mean. I can't live without you. I'm going on leave soon. I'd been going to ask if you would come with me, as my fiancée. I'm longing for you to meet my parents. I know they'd adore you."

They were almost the selfsame words which Susan had used not long ago. She could picture the Reverend Mr St Clair. He would be pale, aesthetic, a gentler version of Geoffrey Forman. His wife, Adelaide, would be a perfect complement to him. She, too, would be a less forceful character than Stephen's mother. She would not have been forever producing hearty pearls-and-twin-set young women in the hopes of finding her son a suitable wife. Mrs St Clair would rely on John's own good judgment, certain that he would bring home some girl like Susan Buckley. Rose could even picture the St Clair home. Rectories were almost all alike: large, old-fashioned, freezing in winter and hopelessly inconvenient. There would only be one lavatory with a wide mahogany seat at the end of some long passage, a bathroom for which some kind of timetable for ablutions was arranged, the wishes of visitors always taking preference. And the rectory garden would be bound to be full of weeds, with an uneven tennis court covered in daisies and a fruit cage, which never wholly kept out the birds. Poor Mrs St Clair would be constantly inside it during the summer months, trying to cope with sodden strawberries and mildewy blackcurrants.

"John," she said, slowly. "I think you are being far too precipitate. As I told you before, we're almost strangers. And I couldn't possibly get leave to coincide with yours. We're still on semi-alert because of the Battle of Britain."

He looked like a small boy who had been temporarily thwarted. "But you didn't say 'No'," he persisted.

As she wished him goodbye, she realised that was true. She hadn't said 'No'. Why?

Later that night, as she lay listening to the snores of her companions, she knew why she had not let him give up hope. The subconscious impulses which so often governed her actions had a nasty way of catching up with her later on and explaining themselves with chilling clarity. She was not at all pleased with what she now knew to be correct. She was, in fact, deeply ashamed. But there was no denying it. If she married John St Clair and quickly became pregnant, it would be an escape from the A.T.S.

20

Rose Delafield and John St Clair were married in the last week of October, a month that had come in raw and rough. John's father, Ronald, officiated at the ceremony in the small parish church at Kinton, where the congregation was made up entirely of St Clair friends and relations, who mostly lived in the neighbourhood.

If Ronald and his wife thought it strange that Rose had no one on her side to support her, to their credit they did not show it. They knew she had been an only child, whose parents were both dead, and this had aroused their deep compassion. Besides, with the war on, it was generally accepted that travelling any distance—especially for purely social occasions—was difficult.

The only two people whom Rose felt she might have liked to attend her wedding were Elena Scholte and, somewhat ironically, Susan Buckley. But Elena, now crippled with arthritis, went nowhere these days. She had refused to leave her home when the bombing of London started in earnest at the beginning of September, maintaining she was not at all afraid. If a bomb scored a direct hit on the house with her inside it, then she would be joining Carl that much sooner. This was where she had lived for many years, where all her memories and treasures lay, and this was where she wished to die.

As for Susan, because she was now on a gruelling course at an O.C.T.U. in Edinburgh, she too was unable to be present. But she wrote Rose a ten-page letter managing to combinbe regret, congratulations, good wishes of every description, compliments to John on his cleverness in finding such a perfect wife-to-be, and ending with a typically naïve but sincere paragraph in which came the words: "I can't help feeling I shall miss the *unmarried* Rose, if you see what I mean, more than I can say. But I do hope I'll get to meet the *married* one again soon, *and* her husband, even if we won't have a chance to have any more maidenly heart to hearts."

Rose thought she would scarcely have described their conversations as such, but at least, by marrying, she hoped it would put an end to Susan's dog-like devotion. A week later, she received an antique silver Apostle spoon from the girl. She realised it must have cost her a fortune. She felt like weeping: for Susan, for herself and for John.

The five-day honeymoon was to be spent at a guest-house called Riversmead, just outside Oxford, known to the St Clair family, after which John was to rejoin his regiment at Weston-super-Mare and she would return to Hemmings. He had confided to her, shyly, that he had always imagined spending part of his honeymoon in London, either at the Dorchester or the Savoy, but they both realised that, with the blitz at its height, this would hardly be desirable, even if they could have afforded it—which was doubtful. Rose, however, was definitely not looking forward to the guest-house, where apparently her future in-laws had stayed when John had been at Magdalen. Yet she felt that she was in no position to demur.

They arrived there during a torrential downpour, in the late evening after the wedding, driven by taxi from the station. It was difficult, in the black-out, to discern what sort of a building it was but, once inside the dimly-lit hall, Rose's worst fears were confirmed. It seemed to be a typical English rectory all over again.

They were shown up to a room with a brass-railed double bedstead covered by a greyish-white lace overlay. There was one faded chintz-covered arm-chair, another upright one, a heavy mahogany wardrobe and a chest of drawers. The curtains were red velvet which had seen better days. She shivered slightly. The room was not only cold but smelt musty and damp. She knew that John was desperately disappointed, but doing his best not to show it.

"You must be so tired, darling. You need sustenance. The lady at the desk said we should go down to the dining-room at once. Is that all right? I'll go on ahead and order something to drink. Perhaps you could meet me there in a few minutes."

"Yes, I shan't be long."

She took off the fur coat which she had managed to extract from her belongings stored with Elena and regarded the top half of herself in the mirror above the chest of drawers. She had explained away the possession of the fur to the St Clairs—as well as the becoming, if out-of-fashion, beige angora Molyneux dress she was wearing—by saying that she had bought them with a small legacy left her by her late Aunt Jackson, who had stipulated that it must be spent on something wholly frivolous that she would never normally buy. Rose had been surprised at how easy such a sudden fabrication had come to her mind. She recalled the indulgent look Adelaide St Clair had given her, as she said, "You did quite right, Rose. You have excellent taste. I'm sure your aunt would be delighted that you put the money to such splendid use and your purchases came in so handy at the time of your wedding."

When she arrived in the dining-room, Rose was touched to find that there was a bottle of champagne in an ice-bucket on the table. She smiled and thanked John, albeit acutely aware that the remaining diners were looking discreetly in their direction and then back at each other again. She knew what they would be saying: newlyweds. She drank the first glass the waiter poured out for her almost at a gulp.

In the lounge, after a dinner of Windsor soup, liver cutlets and trifle, as she felt the effects of the champagne beginning to wear off, she said, "I think I'll go to bed now," to which he replied, nervously, putting down his coffee-cup, "I'll give you half an hour, shall I?"

It was a half-hour in which she felt singularly ill at ease. She had sometimes wondered what would happen if and when he discovered that she was not a virgin. But until now she had been able to dismiss the thought, because he seemed altogether too innocent to know anything about the female anatomy. And, if the worst came to the worst, she reckoned on there always being plausible excuses: she remembered reading somewhere that hymens could be broken by doctors' examinations, or through youthful accidents at games. Even so, now that the moment had all but arrived, she prayed that

no dissembling would be necessary, that he would be too
carried away, that passion would blind him to all other
considerations.

But, after she had bathed and put on a pretty crêpe-de-
Chine nightdress—which she reckoned could also be attri-
buted to Aunt Jackson's legacy—and John was at last in bed
beside her, any uncontrollable urge which had once been so
manifest in the meadows at the back of Eresby House seemed
entirely lacking. When she turned towards him and sought his
hand, she found him trembling. She felt it was a pity they
were in the dark. He had scarcely looked at her or her
nightdress before switching off the light, almost as if he
wanted to hide, to escape from the compromising position in
which he found himself. She realised that it was up to her to
take the initiative.

"John. Aren't you going to kiss me?"

His lips found hers and she parted them slightly,
remembering how it had excited him before. For a little while
she sensed that her tactics were succeeding. She felt his body
harden against hers. Then, to her consternation, he appeared
to break away, fumbling for something on the bedside table.
She could have kicked herself for not realising that he would
try to take precautions, consider he was responsible for
contraception. It was something they had never discussed. He
had only said, "Sometime, when the war's over, I hope we'll
have a baby, a little girl just like you."

The present interruption to their lovemaking obviously
distressed him. Unable to manage to put on a sheath, they
resumed kissing. After a while, she deliberately dropped one
of her hands and let it stray inside his pyjamas, while trying to
guide one of his own beneath her nightdress. He became
aroused at once but, with infuriating perseverance, he once
more tried to put on a sheath. After two further attempts, as if
by mutual consent, they abandoned any thought of
consummating the marriage that night.

On the last day of their honeymoon, the same state of affairs
still existed. The rain, which had attended their wedding day,
never seemed to let up. Clad in mackintoshes and armed with
umbrellas, they went for long walks or played billiards in a

room at the back of the guest-house. One afternoon, they went to the pictures in Oxford and saw Charles Boyer and Irene Dunn in *When Tomorrow Comes*, after which they ate a late tea at a Lyons Corner House.

"I don't," she said, on returning, "feel much like a dinner tonight after all that food, do you?" She was kneeling in front of the small gas fire in their room, which seemed to eat up coins at an alarming rate.

"Not particularly."

"Do you think the management would consider sending up a drink and a few sandwiches?"

He looked surprised. "We could try, I suppose. If you like, I'll go down and sound them out."

She took a bath while he had gone and was actually lying on the bed by the time he returned, bearing a tray and explaining that, as long as he had been prepared to do the waiting, the dining-room staff had obliged. This suited her well. At least, they would not be disturbed.

He poured out some wine and came and perched himself beside her. After they had each drunk a glass, she said, "John, it isn't imperative, is it, to take precautions against having a baby. I mean, we are *married* now, aren't we."

He looked momentarily embarrassed. "Yes, but I thought we . . . more or less agreed . . . to wait until the war was over."

"That's what you said. I really wouldn't mind, myself. And . . . well, perhaps I should have mentioned it. A doctor did once tell me that it might be more difficult for me to conceive than most women."

"Why?" He looked plainly alarmed now.

"Oh, nothing serious." She laughed. "Only a question of shape, I believe."

She had not lied this time. The gynaecologist to whom Harvey had initially sent her had actually volunteered this information. "I really wouldn't mind taking a chance, John," she added.

"You wouldn't?"

"No." She sat up, allowing the satin quilted dressing-gown she was wearing to fall open slightly. She had nothing on underneath.

That night Rose St Clair started her pregnancy.

21

It was very hot in the rectory garden at Kinton. Rose sat on a small camp stool in the fruit cage, picking gooseberries. She was eight months pregnant. John was at sea, presumably en route for the Middle East.

"You mustn't tire yourself, my dear," Adelaide St Clair had warned her as she left the house, wearing an old straw hat of her mother-in-law's and armed with a pudding basin. "Just enough for a pie, remember. I know John would want you to take extra care, now that you're so near your time."

Although Rose had become used to Adelaide's quaint old-fashioned expressions, she was invariably irritated by them.

"I shall be quite all right, Mumlaw," she replied. The name of Mumlaw and Dadlaw had been dreamt up by John's father in preference to the formal Mr and Mrs St Clair which, until a few months previously, she had felt obliged to call them.

She had been living at the rectory since January, when she was officially discharged from the A.T.S. It had not seemed so bad while John had still been in England and they had been able to maintain contact but, since his departure overseas, she had found the atmosphere wearying and claustrophobic, even though it was one she had known so well in her youth. But she realised that she had travelled a long way since then—also that she had allowed herself to become trapped again, trapped this time by marriage, by a body which daily became more swollen and cumbersome and the well-meaning care of two people to whom she knew she should be grateful, but who at times made her feel like screaming. She was continually, as today, having to pretend.

Sitting at the end of the line of bushes under the hot June sun, she was relieved that at least the baby, who had been kicking violently until a few days ago, seemed to have decided to quieten down. Listlessly, she felt for the hard green berries, hoping that Adelaide had sufficient sugar not to produce an almost inedible pie. Occasionally, she dropped her hands in her lap and let them lie motionless by the basin, while her thoughts strayed in other directions.

They were strange thoughts for a young woman in her position, often going back to her previous lovers and wondering exactly how she had come to be where she was. She did not think much about her husband or the war. She was vaguely aware that clothes rationing had now started and that Germany, for some unknown reason, had turned on Russia, meaning that it would be much easier these days to spend a honeymoon in London where the blitz, at least for the time being, had ceased. London made her think of Elena and the fact that she owed both her and Susan a letter. But she had never been much of a correspondent and, somehow, with the baby on the way, she had felt able to put off such matters. Pregnancy had helped to divorce her from her obligations, from reality. She sensed that her parents-in-law were disappointed in her, but she seemed powerless to do anything about it. If, occasionally, guilt crept into her thoughts, especially concerning the manner in which she had married their son, nowadays inertia acted like a tranquilliser and prevented it having much effect.

About imminent motherhood, she thought hardly at all. Adelaide St Clair had helped her to accumulate a fairly practical layette. In fact, the older woman had seen to most of it, taking the greatest pleasure at the prospect of her grandchild's arrival which, according to the doctor, should now be in five weeks' time. Both women hoped the baby would be a girl, because that was what John had wanted and Rose herself, knowing nothing about small babies, felt it might be easier for her to relate to one of her own sex. A farmer's wife in the village had lent her a book on child care, but she had only briefly glanced through it. She reckoned that there would always be her mother-in-law in the background. After all, Adelaide had produced John, although how she could have gone through the motions leading to his conception, Rose could not possibly imagine.

Presently, she heard her name being called. There was the

sound of the rickety cage door being opened and then Adelaide stood before her in a shapeless cotton frock and flat brown sandals, a worried expression on her face.

"Rose dear, are you all right? I'm sure you shouldn't be sitting in this heat any longer." She glanced at the half-empty pudding basin. "Never mind about the gooseberries. We can have a pie another day. Do come inside now."

Rose got up awkwardly and followed her mother-in-law into the house. She had been unaware that she had been sitting in the cage so long. It had seemed quite a pleasant way of passing the morning, especially with the baby so quiescent.

"If I were you I'd go and put your feet up now, dear," Adelaide said, as they reached the back door. "I've drawn the curtains in your room and it's still fairly cool. When we go to the hospital for your check-up on Friday, I thought I might try to see if I could buy one of those venetian blinds. I've occasionally seen them in that second-hand shop. We could get old Bert, down at the forge, to fix one up. It'll be a help, too, when the baby comes."

"That's very kind of you, Mumlaw."

She went upstairs and lay down. It seemed easiest, these days, to do what she was told, to let Adelaide assume responsibility. Presently, she dozed.

The following Friday afternoon, she waited for her examination at the hospital in much the same accepting mood, sitting alongside several other pregnant women in a small stuffy ante-room. When she was eventually seen by a lady doctor whom she had not encountered before, she was slightly surprised to be asked if she had anyone accompanying her that day.

"Yes. My mother-in-law. She'll be calling back to collect me."

"What time?"

"About three-thirty, I think." She could visualise Adelaide, now busily poking around in some junk shop.

"I should like to see you both when she comes. Perhaps you would wait outside."

The flat expressionless voice seemed to protect its owner from being asked any questions at that moment, but Rose felt uneasy as she went back to the airless room, where she sat staring at a pile of old tattered magazines and a newspaper dated a month previously, reporting the extraordinary arrival of Rudolf Hess, who had descended by parachute from a German plane on to Scottish soil. When Adelaide, hot and flustered, appeared at the door and Rose explained that they had both been asked to wait, it was impossible to ignore the look of terror which crept into the older woman's eyes, the way a deeper red suffused her whole face and neck. Ever since she had known her, Rose had supposed that John's mother was going through the change of life, but so far she had merely thought of it as no concern of hers. Now, it suddenly occurred to her that as Adelaide's anxiety was so obviously much greater than her own she should try to show a little more consideration.

"Do sit down, Mumlaw. It'll do you good to have a rest. I'm sure it's nothing. They probably just take extra care at this stage."

But when they were summoned into the doctor's room, they found she was not alone. They were introduced to a Mr Fanshaw, the senior gynaecologist. Rose was then subjected to a further examination. When she was once more dressed and they were all seated round the desk, he said, looking straight at Rose, "I am very sorry, but I have bad news. My colleague here and I can no longer detect a heartbeat. I should like to admit you straight away for investigation under anaesthetic."

It was Adelaide who answered, her words no more than a whisper. "The baby . . . you mean . . .?" She was unable to go on.

He nodded. "Yes. I fear . . . there is every reason to think it will be stillborn. Your daughter-in-law has explained that she has actually felt no movement all this week."

Adelaide put up a hand to her face. "I should never," she said, her voice now almost inaudible, "have let you pick those gooseberries on Wednesday."

Mr Fanshaw did his best to comfort her. "Please don't blame yourself, Mrs St Clair. The baby must have been dead for several days."

Rose heard them discussing her plight, but as if from a long way off. It was an odd sensation. She did not feel particularly grieved. When the time came for the anaesthetic, she could only feel relief that she would no longer have to carry around such a weight and, although it was only a very fleeting thought as a needle was plunged into arm, relief that she would not, after all, have the business of caring for a small baby.

Owing to the shortage of beds and out of compassion for her seemingly tragic situation, she was put in a private amenity room at the end of the maternity wing. The nurses were kind but either very young or elderly, the latter having come out of retirement to do what they could in the national emergency. All seemed equally embarrassed and concerned for Rose, when the cries of a new-born infant could be heard or when a passing mother could be seen above the partly glass walls, carrying some small bundle in her arms.

Yet it was the older St Clairs who were so manifestly the more distressed when they came to visit their daughter-in-law the following afternoon. It was plain that Adelaide had been crying and Ronald, though used to visiting the sick or grieving, seemed somehow now to be out of place, at a loss for words. Only when they got up to go did he grip Rose's hand tightly and send up a short prayer. She wanted to respond to them both, knew that she ought to, but their very goodness in the face of what, deep down, she knew to be her own treachery made it an impossibility. A grandchild would have meant so much to them, made up for their son's absence. It seemed all the worse, because the baby had been a little girl, what John had wanted. That night, for the first time since she had received Susan Buckley's wedding present, Rose wept.

She returned to the rectory after a few days and recovered, physically, in a comparatively short time. She was given certain drugs to dry up the milk supply and by August her astonishingly good figure was back to normal. She could scarcely credit that she had ever been pregnant.

There were others in Kinton who also noticed the emergence of a new, svelte Rose. Having come to Kinton already three months pregnant and well-wrapped up in winter clothes, this extremely attractive young woman who could often be seen walking through the village with the St Clairs' old cocker spaniel caused several heads to turn. When, at the beginning of September, she appeared in George Lorrimer's harvest field, wearing trousers and a man's shirt, with her shoulder-length hair drawn back by an emerald green chiffon scarf, there was more than mere head-turning. There was talk.

Adelaide St Clair had done her best to prevent Rose asking George Lorrimer at the Manor Farm if he could do with an extra hand. "For one thing, my dear." she had said, "it is far too *soon*. And no one will expect you to take part in the war effort just yet. You did your bit right from the beginning until your pregnancy. You are the wife of a serving officer. It wouldn't . . . well, it isn't *seemly* for you to be seen taking up land-work now."

"But I'll only do a few hours each day," Rose had replied. "George is late with the harvest after all that rain we had in August. And . . . well, it would be nice to feel useful for a change." She did not add, "And because I am bored stiff."

But although she had got her way, surprisingly aided and abetted by her father-in-law, who seemed to understand that it was too much to expect Rose simply to remain helping his wife in the rectory all day, neither of them had bargained for the garb in which she set off to embark on an afternoon's harvesting at the Manor Farm. On her return, Adelaide was, for the first time since Rose had known her, positively hostile. In consequence, the atmosphere at supper was painfully tense. The next day she decided to bow to pre-war convention and put on a skirt. It was not nearly so practicable and the stubble chafed her bare legs as she bent to stook.

Coming back in the fading daylight along the dusty road which led to the rectory, Rose wondered how long she could remain in her present environment.

22

By the end of September, George Lorrimer's harvest was safely gathered in, but the season had been poor compared to that of the glorious summer of 1940. He was a good farmer, a good family man and well-liked by his staff. There was little he did not know about the land and its inhabitants in this particular part of England, where he and his forebears had lived for centuries past. Mrs Lorrimer was held in similar esteem. She could always be relied on to help anyone at any time. It was she who had lent Rose the book on child care. She, too, came from farming stock and, promptly at four o'clock every afternoon, had appeared in the harvest field with teas for the workers, which she had prepared in the farmhouse kitchen. Her two daughters, aged twenty and twenty-two, were away in the W.A.A.F.s. Her fifteen-year-old son—for whose youth she daily thanked God, because it seemed reasonable to hope that he would never see active service—was at boarding-school. No scandal had ever touched the Lorrimers. They were straight, open-hearted and widely-respected.

Until Rose.

She had taken to giving Sweep a walk before bedtime each evening. It gave her an excuse to get out of the house. Unlike life inside the rectory, she found that of the village—especially in the twilight—had a salutary effect on her. She wandered along, occasionally noticing a small chink of light from a blacked-out cottage window, telling her much about its occupants: how careful they were and, if it were upstairs, then they were probably of the early-to-bed, early-to-rise kind. Occasionally she passed a local inhabitant, with whom she exchanged goodnights. Quite often, she encountered Bert—whose services had never been needed to erect poor Adelaide's blind—as he came out of the Wheatsheaf. Rose had got to know him well as he, too, had given George Lorrimer a hand with the harvest. Although Bert's jokes were not always in the best of taste, she had struck up a certain rapport with him.

One Sunday evening in early October, she took the lane which ran behind the back of the Manor Farm house and buildings. As she neared the rick yard, she was surprised to see a man who appeared to be working there. On drawing nearer, she saw that he was actually plunging an iron stake into a rick, which she knew had been the last to be made. With a shock, she realised that it was George Lorrimer himself. Memories of her rural upbringing came suddenly to mind. *Of course*—she knew exactly what he was doing. He was testing for overheating. Presently, he straightened up, laid the stake against the wall of the yard and made for the gate, close to where she was standing.

"Is it all right?"

George Lorrimer turned towards her, startled. "Why, *Rose!* Yes, thank God. I couldn't help worrying over this one. We hurried over making it when the weather looked like breaking. I felt I couldn't turn in without seeing all was well. The last thing we want is a fire."

They fell into step. At the gate of the orchard he stopped, raised his cap and wished her goodnight, adding, "I was most grateful for your help, Rose. Thank you again for all you did. And I had no idea you would prove to be such a skilful tractor-driver. If you decide to take up land work, please let me know."

It was a pleasant encounter, no more, no less. She pictured him returning to the farmhouse where his wife, Jean, would be waiting for him. She thought of them going upstairs to bed together. Theirs was an existence—stable, loving and somehow so *right*—which, because she had continued to give in to some inner weakness or flaw in her character, she would never know.

With sadness, she called to Sweep and retraced her steps to the rectory. Although she was aware that her parents-in-law would have retired and trusted her enough to lock up and put the dog into his basket, she also knew that they would never actually settle down and put out the light until they heard she was back or, as her late father might have said "safely within the fold".

That night she lay in bed, tossing and turning, her chance meeting with George Lorrimer still very much in her mind. She wondered if she might take him up on his offer of land work, despite the opposition she would probably have to face from her mother-in-law. Grief, now mingled with a certain resentment, assailed her. She heard the church clock strike eleven, twelve and then every hour until four, after which she dozed, fitfully.

It was not until the end of the month that she saw George again. She was standing at the bus-stop in the local town, having come there one market day to do some household shopping. There had been a time when Adelaide appeared to enjoy such jaunts. But since what she referred to as "the tragedy", she had become not only depressed but curiously absent-minded and withdrawn. Her normally thin figure seemed now no more than a skeleton, draped in ever more shapeless garments. Often, she could be heard muttering to herself, passing her daughter-in-law with a hostile look or even, at times, ignoring her as if she hardly existed. It was, therefore, a relief to Rose to get away and undertake her mother-in-law's one-time job.

But when, on this particularly dismal and wet afternoon, a small truck drew up alongside her and George Lorrimer leant out and called her name, she was delighted at the thought of being given a lift home, thus escaping a dreary crowded bus journey back to Kinton. For all the buses nowadays, as well as being few and far between, seemed to take longer and more tortuous routes, in order that they could serve as many villages as possible. Whereas Rose had been prepared for a journey of about an hour and a half, she realised that it would now be reduced to about forty minutes.

She found, however, that she was a little out in her calculations. They certainly reached the road which ran along the top of the Manor Farm in record time. But here George asked her if she would mind if he drove down to the village through the rough track, which more or less divided his land in half. She was only too pleased. The light was failing but she was interested to see an area into which, so far, even when walking

Sweep, she had never penetrated, all her harvesting work having been done on the lower slopes. These top acres, where mostly sheep grazed, were wild and windswept until, about a mile from the road along which George had driven, they came upon a dip where, hidden from view, lay a cluster of small farm buildings: a skilling, a lean-to and a grander structure which could possibly be classed as a small barn.

"This," George informed her, "is what the locals call Wuthering Depths."

She laughed. "You mean there is water?"

"Too right. There's a dewpond. Been here since time immemorial. I keep a few steers in that fenced-off bit. The stockman looks at them every day, but I always stop by when I can. Would you sooner sit in the truck for a moment? It's pretty nasty outside."

"Oh, no. I'd love to come with you."

She tied the headscarf she was wearing more securely under her chin and walked with him to the back of the buildings, where the steers, their breath steaming in the cold evening air, jostled each other as, inquisitively, they came forward to the fence to meet them. George Lorrimer rubbed the nose of the foremost one with the back of his hand.

"A good bunch this year."

She noticed his practised eye travel over the little herd, missing nothing. Then he continued, "I'd just like to take a look at the hay situation. I'll lead the way, shall I? Watch your step. This path to the barn gets pretty slippery after the kind of rain we've had the last week."

She was wearing a pair of brogue shoes, ones which had been made for her when she was living with Harvey. For some time she had been aware that they needed new soles but had not bothered to do anything about it. She was almost at the entrance to the small barn, when her right foot gave way under her. The next thing she knew was that George was picking her up.

She steadied herself against him while he looked down in some concern.

"Are you all right?"

"Yes, thank you. Very silly of me. You did warn me about

slipping." She put the offending foot to the ground and winced.

"You'd better sit down in here for a while."

He opened the barn door and helped her inside, where she sank gratefully on to a pile of loose hay. She was surprised at the tender and expert way he knelt and examined her foot. "No bones broken, I think, but I'll try to get the truck closer so you won't have to walk further than necessary."

"Thank you, George."

There was a small silence in which she became acutely conscious of his closeness, the pleasant smell of hay, of a feeling that she was in some refuge, away from the elements, away from the rectory, away from Adelaide. She was not conscious that she had parted her lips and lowered her eyes, only that it seemed perfectly natural for George Lorrimer to start kissing her.

23

By Christmas, Rose realised that she would have to leave Kinton. It was not that anyone knew about her affair with George—at least, she did not think so. But there were so many other factors against its continuing.

For one thing, their meeting was becoming increasingly difficult and risky. Although, several times, they had managed to arrange returning together in the same way and by the same route as on the initial occasion, winter had now set in. The evenings were dark and the cold had intensified. The barn at Wuthering Depths was hardly the ideal place for lovemaking.

For another, Rose, for all her sins, had never before had an affair with a married man, unless she counted Harvey. But as, long before they met, he had been virtually parted from his wife, she had never felt blameworthy on that particular score. Now, it was different. Jean Lorrimer was a friend, one whom she greatly admired. Guilt might never have been Rose's strong point, but it was well-nigh impossible not to feel it acutely when she was constantly running into Jean in the village or, sometimes, actually going inside her home.

Oddly enough, the fact that Rose had a husband serving in the Middle East bothered her scarcely at all. John had become such a shadowy figure in her life. Quite often, she would feel obliged to look at his photograph in order to remember the young man she had married. Correspondence between them was erratic, several of his letters arriving in a bunch and then, for some weeks, none at all—a state of affairs which she supposed would be the same at his end, even though she never wrote so often or at such length as he did.

John had taken the news about the baby more philosophically than she had expected. He often referred, in an oblique fashion, to their having another when the war was over. He said little about his present circumstances, possibly because of fear of censorship; yet she also sensed that, because he was so full of nostalgia for the life he remembered at Kinton, he was anxious to dismiss the one he was now leading as some kind of temporary aberration. He was continually using such phrases as, "It's wonderful to think of you being at the rectory and supporting the parents. How they must love having you", or "Is dear old Bert still going strong?" and then, perhaps, ending with a phrase such as, "I think about you all so much, and can picture you walking down through the village like a beautiful tawny princess, everyone wanting to talk to you."

Momentarily, after such a letter, she would think: If you did but know. Then she would become angry, angry with him for being so easily deceived, angry at herself for deceiving.

But there was yet a further reason why she knew she could not remain where she was any longer. At the beginning of December conscription of women had been announced. Being married, she supposed she might just have got away with volunteering to work at the Manor Farm without officially becoming a member of the Land Army. But because of her present relationship with its owner, this was obviously an impossibility. She knew she should never have let her affair with George begin. Now, she was in trouble. What had initially seemed something so pleasantly natural that she had scarcely thought of it as wrong, had got out of hand. She had been quite unprepared for passion, for George's increasing infatuation. It was so out of keeping with his character, although when they had last met he had mentioned, not without considerable embarrassment, that the previous year Jean had undergone a serious operation, after which sexual relations between them had been virtually impossible. This had explained a lot. Even so, it did not expiate guilt—for either of them.

She had made up her mind she would go to London, explain to her parents-in-law that she wanted to do something really worthwhile. In a way this was true for, deep down, she had a tremendous desire to turn over a new leaf. She wished to take up a training that was compatible with the war effort, but which would stand her in good stead when the war was over. If, as John's parents might well say, she would then surely revert to being a wife and mother, she would point out that no one knew what the future held, brutal as the implications of such an observation might be. She would mitigate it by remarking that it could be helpful to John to have a wife with some definite qualification. Adelaide and Ronald couldn't possibly quarrel with that. In short, she would tell them that she intended to become a nurse, a proper nurse, not just a V.A.D., such as those angels of mercy at Eresby House whom she had once admired from a distance. This time she was going to make a real effort—for others, as well as herself.

She decided to broach the subject with her father-in-law first. She was never quite sure how Adelaide would react these days—only that she was almost bound to make trouble. Ronald, for all his asceticism, had a certain clear-sightedness, as well as compassion. She had often wondered whether, in fact, he appreciated what was going on around him far more than he ever divulged. She found this to be only too true on the morning when she asked if she might have a word with him alone in his study.

"But of course, my dear."

She watched while he bent down to place another small green log on the totally inadequate fire, after which they sat down, one on either side of it. The temperature in the room was so low that she could see his breath when he spoke.

"What is it, Rose?"

She had meant to lead up to the subject gently, give him time. Instead, she found herself saying, "I want to leave Kinton, Dadlaw."

He inclined his head. Almost she felt there was a look of relief on his face. "When were you thinking of going, my dear?"

"As soon as possible in the New Year."

She was puzzled by his calm acceptance of her news, as if he had been hoping and waiting for it.

"And *where* were you thinking of going?"

"To London," she replied. "I intend to take a nurse's training at one of the big teaching hopsitals."

"I'm glad, Rose."

She stared at him. He had not asked for any reason. "I felt . . ." She hesitated, unsure how to put it to him. After a moment, she said, "Well, I don't think perhaps I'm doing enough here. I would be doing more good this way. I hope you understand."

His eyes met hers. Before he even spoke she knew that he knew of her predicament.

"I think you have chosen well, Rose. My prayers will go with you. Naturally, it was nice to feel, earlier this year, that we were of help to you and vice versa. Adelaide's health, as you know, has lately been giving me cause for concern. Under any other circumstances, I might have hoped you would remain with us, doing war work but from under our roof."

She did not speak.

Presently, he went on, "Jean Lorrimer came to see me the other day."

She felt her whole body tighten. Her hands gripped the arms of the old wing chair in which she was sitting, waiting for his next words.

"If you had not come to me with this suggestion of going away, it was one I was going to make to you."

"You mean . . . she *knows?*"

"She has known for the past two months, Rose."

There was silence except for the fire, where the damp log lay sizzling in the grate. Outside the window, now that the panes had defrosted, she could see the roadway leading up to Wuthering Depths.

"These are abnormal times, Rose," Ronald St Clair continued. "I lay no blame. I am well aware of the difficulties within the Lorrimer marriage. Jean is a most courageous and understanding wife. And your own husband has been thousands of miles away for almost a year now. I am continually reminded of St Matthew, Chapter 26, verse 41: the spirit indeed is willing but the flesh is weak."

She recalled with startling clarity the day when her own father had uttered the selfsame words. She said nothing, wondering whether her father-in-law would still show so such forgiveness and compassion if he had known of her previous lovers.

"Naturally one regrets," she heard him say, slowly, "but you have made a wise choice, I am sure. And I am grateful, so very grateful, that it has come from you, that you have taken the initiative. I will tell Adelaide of your decision although, of course, not the entire reason for it. I do not think she will be as upset as you might imagine. Nursing has always appealed to her. She had just started her own training when we married."

"Thank you," she said, at last. "I don't feel I deserve such understanding."

He smiled. "You must not forget, my dear, that just because a man takes holy orders, it does not necessarily divorce him from the rest of the world or make him the arbiter of other people's morals. So many people seem to think that parsons belong to another species, that a dog-collar brands them as much as, say, a head-dress on some Indian chief."

She had a sudden desire to reveal her past, to tell him about Harvey, Stephen, Henry and the shameful way she had used his son. But she knew she could not do that. Nevertheless, his words made her all the more determined to try to make good.

24

"For Christ's sake, go easy with the Lysol. It's all very well for Sister Ponsonby to want this place as sterile as an operating theatre, but she'll create merry hell if we use more than a thimbleful. She'll come in and say, 'Don't you know there's a war on?', silly old cow."

Rose and another probationer by the name of Marlene Stacey were cleaning bed-pans in the sluice-room attached to a ward called Pembroke, which dealt with gynaecological complaints. Marlene had been nursing for six months, Rose for three weeks.

"What ever made you take it up, this job?" Marlene enquired, banging a bedpan on to a rack as if it might have been some saucepan. "I shouldn't 'ave thought you'd be the type." She was a small red-headed cockney, cheerful, tough and outspoken.

Rose hesitated. "I . . . just thought it seemed a good thing to do."

"But you're married, aren't you. Where's your hubby?"

"Overseas. The Middle East."

"No kids?"

Again she hesitated, but decided there was no point in going into details. "No," she replied.

"I see. Still, all the same, I'd 'ave thought the likes of you would 'ave joined the Red Cross. We've 'ad a few of 'em 'ere. All dressed up. Posh. Not that they didn't work. Some of 'em gave me quite a surprise. But some'ow you don't expect your kind to be cleaning bed-pans alongside me. Where d'you come from?"

"I . . . was brought up in Norfolk. My father was a parson there."

"Ah! That explains a lot, that does. I suppose you 'ad a call. I don't go much for dog-collar chaps, but there's a good 'un wot comes in 'ere an' says a few prayers when a body's on the way out, like. Sunday nights he takes the service in the ward. For Christ's sake, remember to put screens round the bed if someone calls for a b.p. in the middle of it. I remember that was when I made my first bloomer. You should 'ave 'eard wot the Sister said afterwards. I was on men's surgical then. That seemed to make it worse. Wot d'you do on yer day off?"

"Not . . . a lot. On Thursday I'm going to visit an elderly friend in Hampstead."

"Ain't you got anyone else?"

"No."

"I'd ask you back to my place, down Battersea way, only I don't think you'd care for it much. Our street fair copped it in the blitz. Our 'ouse is about the only one still standing. Thank Gawd 'itler's laid off now, although you never know."

"Did you have bomb victims here?"

"I believe so, but I never came till after the worst was over. I 'ad to be eighteen. I'd 'ave liked to join the Wrens, but I felt that sorry for Mum. Dad and me two brothers are all away in the forces. She needs me to 'ang on to. I go back 'ome whenever I can. It don't take all that long on a Number 46 bus."

When the sluice-room was at last looking as clean and tidy as they felt possible, Rose accompanied Marlene back to the ward, where they were instructed to start the evening bed-making. During their absence there had been another admission, a patient who, as they drew nearer, Rose was sure she had seen before. As the bed in which the woman was lying had not yet had time to become disarranged, they were about to pass on to the next when someone whispered, "Miss Delafield." Rose stopped and turned. It was the voice more than anything which helped her to name its owner, for the face staring at her from the pillow was skeletal, that of a sufferer who, beyond doubt, was—to use Marlene's expression—on the way out.

Rose went up to the bed and put out a hand. "Mrs Corbett!"

She had paused no more than a second, but it was enough. There was the sound of hurried feet. Sister Ponsonby was beside her.

"You are meant to be bed-making, Nurse, not standing about, chatting."

"I'm sorry, Sister, but . . . I happen to know this patient."

"That makes no difference. Hurry along. We are short-staffed this evening." Officiously, Sister Ponsonby turned on her heel and went back down the ward.

With a mixture of sadness and resentment, Rose caught up with Marlene and resumed her allotted task. Would she, she wondered, always place herself in some hopelessly subordinate position? What was it about her that made her constantly get into situations where other women would bully her? Or, for that matter, into quite different situations where men could make love to her? It hardly seemed fair, now that she thought she had done the right thing, for once, and was determined to go straight, improve herself, look to the future and forget the past. Although so far she hadn't been very successful when it came to George Lorrimer. He was still uppermost in her thoughts.

She had managed to tell him, coming out of church on Christmas morning, of all times, that she would be leaving Kinton within a week. She recalled the look of anguish on his face, how at the lych-gate he had raised his hat and said barely audibly, "Goodbye, Rose," before catching up with his wife. She wondered how she could avoid going back to Kinton when she was given a break. It would be difficult not to, but even more difficult if she went. Her only course now seemed to be to apply herself to the job in hand, to endeavour to make a success of it, however humiliating and rigorous the initial training. But whatever happened, she resolved somehow to have a few words with the butler's wife, who had once looked after her in Harvey's London home.

The opportunity came sooner than she expected. The following morning, when Sister Ponsonby was off duty, Rose was asked by the staff nurse—a much more agreeable type—to help her get Mrs Corbett ready for the operating theatre. For a few moments, she found herself alone with the patient behind some screens, while Nurse Fawley went away to prepare an injection.

She wasted no time. Once more putting out a hand she said, "It's so nice to see you again, Mrs Corbett."

"Nice to see you, Miss."

The voice was weak but it was the eyes which Rose found so disturbing, lack lustre, devoid of hope. She made an effort at brightness, but even as she spoke Rose cursed herself inwardly for hypocrisy. "We must get you well and out of here, Mrs Corbett. Very soon."

The woman in the bed said nothing. She knows, Rose thought. And she knows that *I* know. "Your husband," she ventured. "I expect he will be coming to see you later on." Again, she could have kicked herself for insensitivity and lack of imagination, as she listened to the reply.

"Dead, Miss. A stroke not long after . . . well, you know, Mr Frayne passed on."

"I'm terribly sorry. Where are you living now?"

"With my sister-in-law. We don't get on really, but beggars can't be choosers. Not that Mr Frayne wasn't most generous to us all in his will. It's just that I'm not much good living on me own."

Rose felt suddenly glad that Harvey had done right by his servants, even though he had cut her off so ruthlessly. She was about to ask whether Mrs Corbett had kept in touch with the Robsons, but the return of Nurse Fawley, this time frowning, prevented any further conversation. Perhaps, like Sister Ponsonby, she considered Rose was doing too much chatting.

The next day, being her only off-duty one of the week, she went to visit Elena. If she had been shocked by Mrs Corbett's appearance, she was much more shocked by Elena's, even though the latter was not, as yet, in hospital. But she was so obviously lonely and in pain, moving with the greatest difficulty back into the drawing-room after answering the front door-bell. This was a travesty of the soignée effusive woman whom Rose remembered coming to Wilcot. Physical illness and bitterness at Carl's death had taken their toll. Thin and despairing, she sat huddled in a shawl by the side of a small electric fire in a room which showed every sign of neglect. Only *Portrait of Rose* above the mantelshelf gave it any semblance of its one-time elegance.

"Whatever made you come to London and take up nursing?" Elena darted Rose a look of disapproval, almost dislike.

It was the second time she had been asked that question

within the last forty-eight hours. Why, indeed, had she come to London to nurse? To get away from George Lorrimer. But she couldn't tell Elena that. To get away from her mother-in-law? No, that was not enough reason, although it was certainly a relief not to have Adelaide's sad, disturbing presence around all day. To atone for all her past misconduct? That was more like it, but she couldn't say that either. She could only fall back on what she had told Marlene, hoping it didn't sound too pompous.

"I just thought it would be a good thing," she replied. "And you never know. A nurse's training might be useful when the war is over."

"Over? And when do you think that might be? Oh, I know America's come in now after that disgraceful affair at Pearl Harbor last December. But the Japs are overrunning the Far East like a plague of ants. We've a long way to go yet. Sometimes I wonder why I didn't end it all when poor dear Carl died. What is there left for me now, waiting for the end in this mausoleum of a house that I can't look after and can't get out of, day in and day out?"

It was difficult not to think of Elena's point-blank refusal ever to leave it after she became a widow, but Rose managed to enquire, gently, "Haven't you any help?"

A look of scorn now came over Elena's face. "My *dearr* child, don't you know there's a war on? I've a neighbour who does what she can, but she's not much better off than I am. Blind in one eye and a cataract in the other. Sometimes I think it's as well my poor dear Carl went. How he'd have hated the present conditions."

After making the tea and then washing up afterwards, Rose left her, promising to come again soon. But she knew it would be an effort. She felt infinitely depressed as she sat in the overcrowded bus on the way back to the hospital. Little, painfully clear vignettes kept coming into her mind's eye. She recalled the Christmas of 1935 at Wilcot, when Carl had first caught sight of her in the black velvet dress, how he had said "Don't move", knowing that he wanted to paint her in a certain pose. She remembered the following May, when *Portrait of Rose* was hung in the Royal Academy Summer Exhibition. How exciting and luxurious life had been then. When had it started to go wrong? When Stephen had come on the scene or long before that, when she had first met Harvey himself? If that had not happened would she, perhaps, now be a respectable wife—and even mother?

With horror, she realised she was forgetting that she was, at least married, that she had a husband who trusted in her, and had no idea that she had slept with other men before and now, regrettably, after their marriage.

When she arrived at the nurses' home and was told by Marlene that Mrs Corbett had not survived her operation, she felt quite unable to face going into the dining-room for supper. Instead, she did something she had been in the habit of doing at Kinton, although here the surroundings were not nearly so attractive. She simply went out into the nearby streets and started walking.

25

It did not occur to Rose that, by a strange coincidence, she had come alone to London at the same time as American troops were arriving in England by the thousand. She took, in fact, little interest in the war, beyond how it affected her personally. She had disliked the A.T.S. intensely, partly because of the regimentation and cramped quarters, partly because of a feeling she was looked on as suspect by her superiors as well as contemporaries, and partly because it seemed all so unfeminine and impossible—except on leave—to get out of wearing the hideous khaki uniform, however much she had done to make her own a better fit.

True, the quarters at the nurses' home in which she was now living were no better. It was also true that those in authority acted in the most merciless and inhuman way towards the staff under them; but, probably because of this, she had at least been able to strike up some kind of rapport with other probationers who, however different their age and background—amd she had been surprised and pleased to find that a few came from a similar one to her own—were united by mutual sympathy against daily attacks from their superiors. And for Rose there was also some consolation in the fact that she could occasionally wear ordinary clothes, not that she had bothered to do so until today, when making her visit to Elena.

Now, however, as she turned up the collar of an old but one-time extremely fashionable and expensive top-coat, and once more set off into the black-out, she was not aware of what she was wearing or where she was going or, even, that it had started to snow, so great was her horror of all she had witnessed during the past twenty-four hours. As nothing else—not even Harvey's or Stephen's death, nor guilt at her own lamentable behaviour which was never far from the surface—had ever affected her quite so deeply. She had suddenly come up against old age, in all its stark uncompromising reality.

Common sense told her that she herself had still a long way to go but, nevertheless, it was there, somewhere ahead, a yawning chasm, hideous and lonely. There would come a time when she was no longer beautiful, when men no longer desired her, when her body failed her, withered and semi-paralysed as Elena's or riddled with cancer like Mrs Corbett's. She shivered as she walked over Westminster Bridge. She was still shivering when she reached Piccadilly Circus and then Leicester Square where, for some time, she stood huddled in a doorway, wondering what to do.

"You in trouble, lady?"

An American serviceman stopped before her, drew himself up and saluted smartly. His whole manner and bearing was so confident, his uniform so impeccably clean and neat that she took it he must be an officer. When she did not at once reply, he peered at her more closely out of direct and concerned-looking brown eyes.

"Say, you seem mighty cold. How about coming next door and letting me get you something to warm you up?"

She followed his gaze as he turned his head slightly to the left. She had been quite unconscious that she happened to be standing next to a public house. With a kind of mute childish acceptance she allowed herself to be gently propelled through some doors and then past a heavy curtain, to be confronted by a throng of people so tightly packed that her companion had to fight his way to a corner, where he commandeered a seat for her by explaining to its female occupant, "This lady's sick."

It took him so long to fetch her a drink that she began to wonder whether he had simply dumped her there and left, but at last she saw him wending his way back through the crowd, finally putting into her hand a glass with the admonishment, "There, drink it up. The landlord tried to make out he'd run out of brandy but when I said it was for medicinal purposes, he obliged."

Dutifully, she did as she was told, the first sip reminding her vividly of her visits to Henry's cottage when he, too, had considered she needed warming up.

"It's very kind of you," she managed to say, at last. "Thank you." As he stood beside her, she noticed that he appeared to be drinking beer, a beverage which, owing to the scarcity of all alcohol, she knew to be heavily diluted.

"It's not kind at all," he remarked. "You seemed all done in. I hope there's nothing seriously wrong."

"Wrong? Oh, no. Not really. I just happened to have had some bad news about two . . . old friends. One died and the other is alone and very incapacitated."

"Say! That's terrible."

She wondered how he could seem so genuinely sorry for someone he had only met a quarter of an hour before. At the same time, she noted that he appeared to be studying her, evidently puzzled to have found a well-dressed woman standing alone in a doorway in Leicester Square on a freezing January night. The drink was beginning to have an effect now and she volunteered, "I can't think what I'd have done without this. You've saved my life."

He drew himself up again in mock obeisance. "Only too pleased, ma'am. Private Elmer Burke of the United States Army. And you?"

"Rose," she replied and then, "Rose Delafield," for some reason automatically adopting her maiden name before continuing, "I'm a nurse at a hospital on the other side of the river."

"A *nurse*. Gee! That's great. I envy your patients, lucky men."

She smiled. She was beginning to feel almost human again. "I'm nursing women at the moment. It's a general civilian hospital."

"Say! Is that so? I congratulate you. Back home in Denver my kid sister wants to be a nurse. But Ma and Pa aren't all that keen. It's a hard life, isn't it?"

"I suppose so. I hope I'll stay the course."

Now that she had revived, she knew that he had noted the fact that she wore no wedding ring, something she had tucked away in a box since taking up her new job. She also sensed that he had taken in quite a lot about her during their brief encounter. Feeling it was time to make some kind of retaliation, she asked, "And what about you? Where are you stationed?"

"Right here. London. I'm a clerk working for some of the

top brass. Several of us are billeted in a part called Chelsea. I
just love your little old country. It means something to me.
I've got ancestors who came from somewhere near Oxford.
I'm hoping to spend some leave there. But just for now,
whenever I can, I take a walk. Like tonight, even though
there's not much you can see in the black-out. But it's sure
brought me a bonus, meeting you. Say, you wouldn't like
something to eat, would you? I should have asked before.
There's a club for G.I.s not far from here. How about it?"

"I . . ." She looked at her watch, surprised to find it was
getting on for nine thirty. "I'm sorry," she went on, "but I
must go. We're supposed to be in by ten, unless we have a
special pass."

"Gee! Is that so? Well, the least I can do is to escort you
back. And look, in case you're hungry . . ." he began
searching in the pocket of his uniform, "you might care for a
little candy when you get in. I believe this sort of thing's in
short supply over here."

She thanked him once again, disarmed by his kindness and
sincerity. On the way back to the hospital they stopped for a
few minutes on Westminster Bridge. It was no longer snowing
but, in the moonlight, the black and white scene had taken on
a magical unreal quality. "Beautiful," she heard him murmur,
and then, "it must have been terrible, in the blitz. Were you
here then?" "No," she replied. "No, not then."

She was thankful he did not press her for further answers
and they walked on in silence until they reached the gates of
the hospital. Then he drew himself up as before, saluted and
held out his hand. "It's been the greatest pleasure meeting
you, ma'am. I should like to think it won't be the only time.
When can I see you again?"

She paused, but only for a moment. She knew it was not
much good suggesting an evening, for she rarely came off duty
until eight p.m. and late passes were not easy to come by.
"Next Thursday," she answered, "I shall have another day
off, but that may not suit you."

"I'll do my darnedest to see it does. I have a buddy, name of
Hucky. He and I have an *agreement*, if you see what I mean.
We often stand in for each other. Suppose I call for you at this

very spot at ten a.m., unless I hear to the contrary? Look . . ."
He pulled out a notebook, scribbled his telephone number on
a sheet which he tore out and handed to her; then, eliciting the
number of the pay-phone in the nurses' home, he wrote that
down also. He was nothing if not efficient.

As she hurried across the courtyard, it occurred to her that if
he did try to contact her, he would ask for Rose Delafield and
get no response. But it was no good worrying. Just at the
moment it was more important to get inside where the clock,
to her consternation, was showing a minute to ten. When she
went across to the desk to sign her name and time of return in
the register, she heard the voice of the Sister in charge, as she
walked across the hallway preparatory to locking up, saying,
"One moment later, Nurse St Clair, and you would have had
to ring for entry and your next day off would have been cancelled. Try not to run things so fine in future."

Once in her room, she found several letters awaiting her on
her bed, all forwarded from Kinton. One was from Susan
Buckley, the other three from John. She knew that it was
almost certainly Marlene who would have put them there. It
was nice of the girl, but, just at the moment, she hardly felt
like opening them. Although John could not possibly yet have
heard where she was and what she was doing, nevertheless any
letter from him invariably left her with a feeling of dismay,
inadequacy and temporarily exacerbated her underlying and
ever-present feelings of remorse. The first which she opened
proved no exception. "My Darling Rose," it began,

*I wonder if it is snowing at Kinton. I remember that it is usually
just about this time of year that George Lorrimer gets anxious about
his sheep up above Wuthering Depths. Do you see much of him and
Jean? I hope so. Such a wonderful pair. I love to think of you
living amongst all the people I was brought up with, especially, of
course, the parents. You have no idea how constantly I picture
you—I think I must have some sort of camera inside my head—
sitting by the fire at the Rectory of an evening or helping Mother in
the kitchen or maybe taking dear old Sweep for a walk.*

*Darling, you mentioned the possibility of doing more war work
in your last letter. Don't overdo it, I beg you. After what happened*

*last summer no one would expect you to, surely. You're too good
and fine a person simply to become some number again, as you were
when I first met you. After all, you are my* wife. *Just by being you,
you do so much good to everyone around* . . .

She did not finish the letter. She simply sat there on the bed,
meticulously tearing it into tiny shreds.

26

"I think it's quite, quite marvellous of you." Susan Buckley's eager face opposite Rose, as they sat in one of the new British Restaurants springing up all over the capital, was having the same effect on her as one of John's letters. It was the beginning of April and the girl had written several times to say that she would be passing through London on leave at that time and would like to see Rose. Eventually, the latter had replied and a brief meeting had been fixed for an afternoon when she was having one of her statutory two hours off duty during the day.

"I don't think my taking up a nurse's training is really all that special," Rose answered, trying to play down Susan's seemingly interminable starry-eyed admiration. "After all, look at you. A fully-fledged subaltern. You'll be a Junior Commander soon."

"But that's not the point. I mean, after . . . well, what happened last summer. It must have been so awful for you. Yet, here you are, tending the sick and not just as an amateur V.A.D. You're doing the thing properly. I bet John's terribly proud of you, isn't he?"

Rose bit into an ersatz egg sandwich, trying to give herself time. "Well, I don't know much about that. I dare say he would have liked me to remain at Kinton. You know, be near his parents. But that's enough about me. Let's hear about you, for a change. Tell me what you do exactly."

"Well, I'm in charge of a platoon, about eighty girls. Most of them are fine, but there's one or two who . . . well, you know, their morals aren't up to much. My C.O. says I must keep giving them pep talks. I think she feels I'll exert some kind of good influence. But I often think they're laughing at me up their sleeves. They know perfectly well I'm pretty innocent. That's what makes it so difficult, trying to get through to them. I imagine they've slept around for ages. I simply don't understand how they *could*, do you, Rose? To go in for that sort of thing before one is married is . . . well, unpardonable, to my way of thinking. How could any man trust a woman again, after he'd found out?"

She could feel the colour sweeping into her face. Hastily, she bent over to where her handbag lay on the floor and made a great play of searching for a handkerchief. At last, straightening up, she said as she glanced at her watch, "I'm sure you're doing very well, Susan. I expect those girls secretly admire you, if you did but know it. Look, I'm afraid I've got to go. I daren't be late back on duty."

"No. Of course not. And my train leaves Waterloo at five, too. I'll tell Mummy and Daddy I've seen you. I'm sure they'll be thrilled to have news. I'll give them your love, shall I?"

"Yes, yes of course." Although, as she spoke, she could not believe that Susan's parents, especially Anne, would want it.

She would have liked to have asked many things such as, "Is Major Massingham still at Larcombe cottage? Do you know the Fishers? What is it like at the Grange these days? What happened to the Robsons? Do you ever see anything of Sir Reginald Farquharson and his wife?" But she refrained. Susan might still belong to that world but she, Rose, had travelled other paths. She had an uncomfortable sense of having taken not one but many wrong turnings since living at Wilcot. She was on her way down while Susan Buckley was so very much on her way up.

Rose watched her slim figure, girdled by a highly polished Sam Browne, disappearing towards Waterloo station. Once, Susan stopped, turned and waved. Then she was gone. As Rose moved off in the direction of the hospital, their brief reunion kept haunting her. Surely the girl would marry soon, wouldn't she? Some decent young man whom she would never let down. She was the English rose type, all right: pretty, naïve, warm-hearted and sexually unaware. Perhaps she would always remain so. Rose could not imagine Susan ever momentarily doing something abandoned. She would never behave like herself.

With relief, she went back on duty. For quite a time now she found that at least the work she was doing provided her with some slight consolation when she felt particularly despondent. But there was something else nowadays which also helped. She had ceased to regard the two hours when she came off the ward at night as a period when it was hardly worth going out. Since taking up with Elmer Burke she had met several other Americans only too eager to claim her attention. If the club to which they all belonged seemed too long a journey—unless she happened to have an early evening when she was free at six o'clock—she would simply go to a public house just across the river where she never lacked the offers of a drink—and often offers of another kind.

There was a time when she might have regretted that most of her men friends were not of the officer class. Even now, had she been associating with British troops, she would probably have preferred the situation to be otherwise. But, somehow, it was so difficult to differentiate between G.I.s and those above them, both in their bearing, dress and even voice, that it hardly seemed to matter.

What did matter was that, one and all, they were extremely generous, for ever producing candy, nylon stockings—a commodity hitherto unknown to English girls—Lucky Strike cigarettes and most important, particularly to Rose, drinks, even if these were often of diluted strength and unpredictable supply. Coming off duty, possibly having seen a patient die or knowing that one would be almost certain to do so in the night, she would hastily fling on a top-coat over her uniform and make her way to a place where she knew she would be welcomed, flattered and where the first sip from the glass placed quickly into her hand would lift her into another world. Often, as the hands of the clock in the ward crept towards eight p.m., she could hardly wait.

Her association with Elmer had been most circumspect at the beginning. He had behaved in an almost impossibly correct way. She had begun to wonder whether he was always like this or whether he felt that it was how he should treat any English woman. But, on seeing Rose's reaction to his more outgoing friends, he soon appeared to lose a few of his inhibitions. She had begun to enjoy leading him on and playing off one American against another. If she was suddenly attacked by twinges of conscience, she knew that these could swiftly be silenced by the alcohol which was now becoming an indispensable part of her life.

One thing she was thankful for was that she had no need to feel guilty about not returning to Kinton on her forthcoming leave, which she was obliged to take in May. Her father-in-law had written to say that his unmarried sister was now living at the rectory because unfortunately his wife's mental health had deteriorated alarmingly. The local doctor thought that it all stemmed from the shock she had received the previous summer, when Rose had produced a still-born child. Adelaide had apparently taken to going round the village peering into perambulators and, on one unfortunate occasion, had actually been found trying to pick a baby up from one. She had become more and more confused, thinking John was about to arrive to ask his mother to look after his little daughter, as his wife was dead. Under the circumstances, Ronald felt that seeing Rose might disturb his wife further and it would be best if any visit was, for the moment, postponed and his daughter-in-law made other arrangements.

Though sorry about Adelaide, Rose was only too relieved to have such a valid reason for making such arrangements. She knew that Elmer was due for some leave and suggested that it might be possible to spend some of it together. He seemed at first startled and then delighted at the proposition. He referred to his idea of tracing his ancestors near Oxford and wondered whether Rose knew of anywhere they might stay—with separate accommodation, he had added, quickly.

Immediately, her mind flew back to her honeymoon but she knew that she could not, would not, mention Riversmead. That would be treachery at its basest. Besides, the place was infinitely depressing. Then another hideous thought struck her. She had never told Elmer that she was married. If they went away together it would be necessary to produce her ration book. Somehow, she would have to break it to him beforehand that she was Rose St Clair. Just why she had reverted to her maiden name when he had asked her, she was still unsure, except that she had the greatest desire to dissociate herself from John.

She chose to make her revelation on a late April evening when they were walking in Hyde Park. Despite the evidence of wartime London, with its dug-outs, sandbags and lack of bedding-out plants, it was still beautiful, the cherry trees cheerfully tossing their pink and white rosettes in the breeze, the wildfowl still plentiful and active on the Serpentine.

For a moment after she had spoken, she wondered whether he had heard her. He remained silent, his eyes fixed on a certain duck preening itself at the water's edge. Then, quite suddenly, he turned the full attention of his strangely intense brown eyes upon her. "I had been going to ask you if you would marry me," he said, "when we were at Oxford. Obviously, I have made some kind of mistake."

He walked away. She began to run after him, then stopped. She knew it was no good. He might be an American but one who belonged to Susan's world. She stood there in the fading daylight, wondering what to do, where she would spend her leave.

In the event, having nowhere else to go, she went to Elena's, caring for an increasingly disabled and irascible old lady.

27

She started losing her figure that summer. The using of different muscles through constantly lifting heavy patients had thickened her waistline, while the wartime hospital food and fairly regular drinking all combined to make her put on at least a stone and a half.

She told herself that she did not mind. She was still attractive to men and having a good time when off duty. Since parting with Elmer, who kept well away from all his previous haunts, she did not lack for admirers and, in some cases, sleeping partners. If her lifestyle now alienated her from her co-workers—rather as in the A.T.S.—she did not mind that either, although she was disconcerted when Marlene, having seen her being escorted by a G.I. one day, said, later on, "You're a rum one. Can't think your hubby would be very pleased, poor bugger, especially as I suppose he was in that retreat from Tobruk."

But along with her increased girth, there was an increase not only in hardness but also self-destructiveness. She began taking risks, going into places which the hospital authorities had placed out of bounds, coming back late and climbing through a small lavatory window at the back of the nurses' home. Inevitably, in due course, she was found out. Sent for by the matron, she stood before her quite impassively, feeling none of the fear which this intimidating woman usually engendered in others. Rose was well aware that owing to wartime exigencies and shortage of staff, she was unlikely to be thrown out, although the curtailment of free time and the cancellation of all late passes for two months certainly cramped her style.

Curiously enough, one thing which never seemed to suffer was her work. She had now become inured to suffering and tragedy. She could lay out a dead body without any qualms, help with an intricate dressing or sudden haemorrhage with calm and efficiency. Often she surprised herself. She seemed to be two different people, laying aside the nurse as she took off her apron.

She received two letters from John in the autumn giving even fewer details about himself or his whereabouts than usual. This was not surprising for, since the disaster of Tobruk, coming after a monotonous procession of evacuations, sieges and defeats, the news was being hushed up both abroad and at home. Her husband appeared far more concerned about why she had not been back to Kinton, especially as he understood from one of his father's letters that his mother had not been at all well. Could not Rose give him some first-hand information? The veiled criticism and disappointment came through with every line. She ignored it and eventually wrote back describing the film, *Mrs Miniver*, which she had just seen.

When Montgomery turned the tide with his victory at El Alamein that November, it was well after Christmas before she heard from John again and, with the speeding up of events in the Middle East, correspondence between them became, of necessity, less and less frequent throughout 1943. With the capture of Tunis all organised German resistance in North Africa ceased and John St Clair's regiment was the first to land on Italian soil.

It dawned on Rose that slowly but surely, barring death or injury, her husband was moving nearer home, that even if, as Churchill put it, it was not the "beginning of the end", it was certainly "the end of the beginning". The Second Front, for which so many people were clamouring, would be bound to take place within a year or so. She could then well be confronted by a young man whom she hardly knew, who would want to take her back to Kinton, possibly even settle down near there and embark on some peacetime career. The thought appalled her. Occasionally, she began having nightmares about it.

At the beginning of 1944, the Luftwaffe turned its attention once again on London. During three months the capital had thirteen major attacks, far more dispiriting after the long lull, than the regular raids had been in 1940. The Germans now

used bigger and more destructive bombs. With the retaliation
of the new rocket guns, the sheer din was unprecedented. The
attacks were short, sharp and concentrated, involving a high
proportion of incendiaries. The Little Blitz, as it soon became
known, also ranged as far as Hull, Bristol and South Wales,
but it was the capital which bore the brunt and in February
alone a thousand people were killed, among them Elena
Scholte.

Rose knew nothing about this for six weeks. Her visits to
Hampstead had become as infrequent and erratic as her letters
to John. Elena's physical state and resentful attitude towards
all and sundry depressed her beyond measure. But, just occasionally, she still made the journey by bus or tube, not so
much to see Elena as to collect some small possession or take
another look at *Portrait of Rose*, even if the reminder of herself
as she had been nearly ten years previously gave her both
pleasure and pain.

On this particular day, there appeared to be nothing different about the road in which Elena lived until Rose rounded
a bend and found herself staring in horror at a patch of rubble
which had once been the Scholtes' home. There was no one
about, a bitter March wind swept across from the Heath, the
daylight was fading. Gradually moving a little closer, she stood
looking down on a heap of bricks covering the one-time floor of
the drawing-room where once her picture had graced the wall.
In a kind of frenzy, she began kicking at them with her foot,
consumed by the irrational thought that *Portrait of Rose* might
still be lying underneath. She was not sure how long she
remained frantically scrabbling about, only that at some point,
she heard a male voice behind her, saying, "There, there,
lady. Best not to take on like that."

She turned, to find an air-raid warden standing by his
bicycle, looking at her in some concern.

"What . . . when did it happen?" she asked.

"Back in the middle of February. We never had all that
many bombs out this way before, but with this new lot we
seem to be a bit more in the firing line."

"And Mrs Scholte?"

"The lady of the house? Was she a friend of yours?"

"Yes."

"She was killed, poor old soul. Direct hit, as you can see. Never suffered, thank God."

"And all her things? What happened to them?"

"Them? Oh, well, you'll have to ask at the town hall about that. It'll be closed now. Might be best to write. We did our best to stop the looting, but it's not always easy."

Dazed, she walked back to the tube station. She wished she had asked the man where Elena had been buried. She began wondering who had buried her? Had she named a next-of-kin? Who was her solicitor? Was there a will? Or was that, too, buried in the rubble so that no one had known what to do, to whom to turn? It occurred to Rose that similar situations must have arisen throughout the war, although she knew of no one who lived a life in quite such a reclusive fashion as Elena, seemingly bereft of friends and relations. Thank God her final passing had been quick. If Rose had been religious she would like to have thought the Scholtes were now reunited—according to Elena's one-time wish. But somehow she could not think that. She might have been a parson's daughter and a parson's daughter-in-law, but she had long ago lost her faith.

The authorities at the town hall took a long time to answer her letter and when they did it simply referred her to a Mr Brandt, a solicitor in Lincoln's Inn, who would doubtless be able to give her the further information she required. Once again, she was forced to wait several more weeks before receiving an answer from him, in which he stated that the Jewish Joint Burial Society had taken care of the deceased's funeral arrangements and that she had altered her will immediately after her husband's death, leaving everything to a Jewish refugee fund. What effects had been rescued from the bomb damage were being sold at a Hampstead auction rooms at the end of May. There was no mention, Mr Brandt went on, of Mrs Scholte having housed any property belonging to another party.

And, of course, there wouldn't be, Rose realised. Carl had suffered his fatal stroke in March 1939, when Hitler had annexed the whole of Czechoslovakia. She had not left anything with Elena until war broke out six months later, by which time she would have made her new will. Rose had never thought to make an inventory or obtain some kind of receipt for her effects or, if she had, it had somehow seemed inappropriate when dealing with a friend. What a fool she had been. She did not mind now about her smaller belongings, but she did mind about the portrait. Had it been damaged beyond all recognition? Buried so deep that it had never been found? Or was it looted? It became imperative to her to have a look at the sale items as soon as possible.

She wrote once more to Elena's lawyer—hardly the most co-operative of types—who wrote back agreeing, somewhat reluctantly, to allow Rose to view the deceased's effects but, without irrefutable evidence of ownership, he explained that he would never be able to pass anything over. He believed the things were at the moment at the back of the store, but he would be prepared to meet Rose there shortly before the day of the sale, when there would be easier access to them.

London seemed singularly quiet and empty when Rose walked over Westminster Bridge early one morning en route for Hampstead during the last week in May. There was almost a hush about the place. The air raids in the earlier part of the year had ceased. The Luftwaffe appeared to have shot its bolt. Everyone knew that the Second Front was imminent but no one—save a very few V.I.P.s—knew exactly how, when or where it was to take place. But all the troops who had thronged the streets and with whom Rose had been consorting suddenly seemed to have disappeared elsewhere. She supposed it was wrong of her to be worrying over a portrait at a time like this, but the desire to find out about it drove her on. A feeling of unreality—possibly heightened by exhaustion having just come off night duty—took hold of her, as well as an appalling loneliness. It was as if she had nothing and no one to turn to, save her own portrait. In some curious way which she could not understand, it provided her with a sense of identity. With every step she took, with every minute that passed, it became more and more important to her to find her youthful image.

But *Portrait of Rose* was not in the Hampstead sale rooms.

28

She began to notice him soon after the Second Front was launched and the doodle-bugs started coming over. She was working in Out-Patients then and this desperate haunted-looking character would sit in the waiting-room every Tuesday and Friday morning, chain-smoking until it was time for him to see the psychiatrist. Despite his obviously nervous state, he was a sturdy, thickset man—dark, with something of the gipsy about him. It occurred to her that he could well have taken the part of Heathcliff in the film *Wuthering Heights*, which she had seen the year war broke out.

There was often little opportunity to glance at any of the patients' notes but on one occasion, as she was clearing up, she managed to take a quick look at the dossier pertaining to Captain Michael James Naresby. On this particular Wednesday, when the sinister grating sound of one of Hitler's flying bombs could be heard faintly in the distance, he had been the first to fling himself to the floor. This was by no means an unusual reaction nowadays, if the growing noise seemed to indicate that the menace would pass anywhere overhead, for everyone knew that it could suddenly cut out, without warning, and crash to earth with an ear-splitting roar, followed by a blinding flash and a tall sooty plume of smoke. Most people however, would wait tensely to see how directly they were in the firing line before abandoning dignity and taking the steps which Michael Naresby had done the moment there had been the slightest murmur from what had become known as Bomb Alley: the route from bases in the *Pas de Calais* via Kent to the capital.

It appeared from his papers that Captain Michael Naresby had been recently invalided out of the army on the grounds of psychoneurosis. The letters L.M.F. were scrawled heavily over the final page from Headquarters, Southern Command. Although Rose's connection with the armed services had been brief, she knew what that meant: Lack of Moral Fibre. She wondered what had happened, what story lay behind the stark type-written sheets, what heredity or upbringing had produced this unfortunate individual who had now cracked under strain, so that he had been unable to take part in D-Day. Just as she was about to close the file, her eyes fell on his present address, a mews house close to where she had once lived with Stephen near Holland Park.

The following Friday she took care to see that Michael Naresby was the last patient to enter the psychiatrist's consulting room. When he came out and they were alone in the waiting-room, something impelled her to say, "Goodbye Captain Naresby. I trust you are feeling better."

He looked startled. It was clear that he had been more or less unaware of her existence. "What made you ask?" he replied, frowning.

She shrugged. "In this department one never quite knows how a patient is getting along. One has so little contact, except through the files. I happened to see from yours that you live in an area in which I also lived just before the war."

"Really? Are you in the habit of carrying out detective work on people's private lives?"

She flushed. Before giving her time to answer, he made for the door, his broad shoulders hunched, the back of his down-at-heel appearance seeming to convey a curt and complete rejection.

She was piqued. Despite her increased weight and sadly deteriorating complexion she had not, as yet, ever encountered such an attitude on the part of any man to whom she had made an overture. This Michael Naresby evidently regarded her with no more interest than he would some stiff, elderly, spinsterish Sister.

The following Wednesday, however, she was surprised to find that he actually acknowledged her presence on arrival and, on leaving, suddenly remarked, "I've been thinking about what you said. Living near me. Would you care to visit the place again?"

"That would be nice. I should like to very much indeed."

"Tonight then. About seven. You've evidently done a recce

on the address."

Once again, he was gone without bothering to wait for a reply. As it happened, working in this particular department meant that all her evenings were free and, as she wanted to find out more about him, both as a patient and as a man, there was no hesitation in her mind about going.

But she was quite unprepared for what she found on arriving at the small mews house. Michael Naresby appeared to be living in squalor. Unwashed crockery littered not just the front room but the whole of the kitchen as well, in which dirty garments were also strewn. The air was thick with cigarette smoke. The only bright spot in the dismal scene which she at once noticed was a hard-to-come-by bottle of whisky, two thirds full, on the kitchen table. From her host's manner, though by no means drunk, she felt he could well have already consumed the other third.

"Like some?" He pointed to the bottle.

"Thank you."

"Water or neat?" He began pouring her a stiff measure into a none-too-clean glass.

"A little water, please."

"Help yourself." He jerked his head in the direction of the tap. "Doc wouldn't like to see me like this, would he?" he continued, as she did as she was bidden and joined him at the table.

"No."

"You haven't come to spy on me, have you?"

"No."

"What made you come, then?"

"You asked me."

"Simple as that, eh? You surely don't *fancy* me, do you? All washed up. Coward of the first degree. Couldn't make it across the Channel. Let 'em all down."

The drink began to have an effect on her. With the absence of so many American troops from the capital, she had not had so much opportunity to be revived in such fashion of late. Suddenly the squalor around her did not seem to matter so much as this man's story.

"What happened?" she asked.

"You've read my notes. Weren't they *enough*? Didn't they *tell* you what happened on the night when Eisenhower held up the whole bloody shooting match because the weather cut up rough?"

"No."

"No?" He folded his arms on the table and laid down his head. A muffled voice went on, "No, I suppose they wouldn't. The great British public hasn't been told the full details yet. That'll be for the history books. And even they won't be able to tell what it was *really* like; how Captain Michael Naresby had been waiting with the assault troops behind a barbed-wire entanglement, cut off from the outside world for weeks, waiting to *go*, you understand. And then, on June 5th, we were all set, under starters', or rather sailing, orders, actually squashed up like sardines in the bloody little craft—only, God, suddenly the order came through: Cancelled."

He raised his head and stared at her out of dark tormented eyes. "I don't know why I'm telling you all this. I don't even know your name."

"Rose."

He appeared not to hear. He was in full spate now. "So, what did Captain Bloody Naresby do? I'll tell you what he did. He went berserk. Literally rocked the boat. They had to hold me down. Prevent me from jumping overboard. Then someone came and gave me a shot in the arm and the next thing I knew I was in hospital at Tidworth. I would have been court-martialled, I daresay, in days gone by. Now, I was simply discharged on medical grounds, flung out as a cuckoo case, referred to the most convenient civilian hospital in the area where I said I would be living. That's where you come in. Have another drink."

"Thank you."

His story both appalled and excited her. She knew she had the power to help this man, even if, at the moment, the awareness was more on a subconscious level than a conscious one. She could visualise him somewhere down near Southampton Water: passionate, quick-tempered and frightened. Unable to show it. All pent up. No release. No woman . . .

"How come you are here?" she asked.

"This place belongs to a friend. He's already out there, poor devil. In the thick of it. Somewhere up front, shouldn't wonder, pushing eastwards, alongside Monty. He always said if ever I wanted a bolt-hole, I could use it. Funny how he hit on the right word, isn't it?"

There was a small silence. Then she said, "I should say your bolt-hole could do with a clean-up, when I come again."

"Are you coming again?"

"If you would like me to. Is the upstairs in just as bad a state as the downstairs?"

She had all his attention now. "Perhaps you'd better come up and see," he replied.

29

As winter closed in that year, Rose embarked on what was to be her most passionate and disastrous affair. In some extraordinary way, the more she saw of Michael Naresby the more his guilt took over from her own guilt. In trying to help him in the only way she knew how, she was able to suppress all the unwelcome thoughts which from time to time assailed her, particularly, nowadays, the one concerning her husband's return and the shameful, unpardonable wish that it might never come to pass.

Rather as she had found nursing to be a silencer of conscience so, in a confused and self-delusory way, the task of caring for Michael Naresby—naturally a much more rewarding and pleasurable one—became her *raison d'être*. She was as obsessed with him as Harvey Frayne had once been with her. At one stage, when Hitler's VIs and V2s seemed to be at the peak of their destructiveness—twenty thousand houses being damaged in the course of a single day—and Michael said something to her about leaving London, she all but broke down, begging him to stay. His reply came as both a shock and a challenge.

"I expect you to come with me."

"*Come with you?*"

"Yes."

"But where . . . how?"

"I don't know. Anywhere. Scotland maybe."

She became suddenly practical. "And what would we live on?"

"God knows. I suppose I might be able to pick up the odd job. And you'd always have your training to fall back on if the worst came to the worst."

In a way, she knew that to be true, for she was now state-registered, but she also knew that if she abandoned her present post at no notice, without references and particularly with the war not ended, she would never be taken on by another hospital.

She had often wondered just what resources Michael did have at his disposal. She supposed he must have *some* money in the bank in order to buy the drink which he craved as his constant solace, although it puzzled her where it came from. Pre-war stocks of whisky were in such short supply now.

One bitterly cold evening towards the end of February she arrived at the mews to find him unusually tense and truculent. Once again, he kept referring to "getting the hell out of it", yet she knew that it could not be the doodlebugs which were getting him down this time, for it was obvious their power to intimidate and destroy was on the wane.

"The war's as good as over, Rose. If you dropped out now it wouldn't be defecting from duty like yours truly. And you know you're dreading meeting your precious husband. Well, here's your chance. We could . . ."

A loud knocking on the front door interrupted whatever further proposition he was about to make. She saw him start, a look of terror come into his eyes such as she had never before witnessed. She got up to answer it but he pulled her back. The grip on her arm made her wince with pain. His other hand motioned her not to speak.

The knocking was repeated and then heavy footsteps could be heard walking back up the mews. It was she who broke the ensuing silence.

"Who did you think it was?"

"The police."

"The *police*?"

"Yes." He poured himself another drink which he downed in almost one gulp.

"Why would the police come here?"

He paused and looked down at the empty glass on the table. Then, suddenly, he jerked up his head and stared her straight in the face.

"Surely you're not *that* naïve, Rose? How do you think I come by this stuff? Ever heard of the Black Market?"

"Of course I have."

"Well, I'm in it. Up to the neck. Not just with the likes of this." He picked up the bottle and poured himself another stiff measure. "There's a hell of a lot of other commodities which people are willing to pay for once they know where to get them. Rubber tyres, for instance. You might call me a middleman, so to speak. You've not been here much in the daytime or you might have met some of my . . . associates. Chap by the name of Trew has been a bloody fool. Sailed too close to the wind. He's hopped it and now that's what I'm going to do. Tonight."

"*Tonight?*"

"Rose, for God's sake, grow up. You don't imagine there won't be further knockings on the door, do you? If not later this evening, then early tomorrow."

She felt panic rising within her. He was proposing something crazy, suicidal, yet she knew she could not bear to let him go alone.

"What about my things?" She had a swift and startling recollection of having said much the same words to Stephen Forman when he had swept her straight off to London in his Hispano-Suiza after the inquest into Harvey's death. But this time there would certainly be no luxury attached to her departure, as Michael's answer made all too plain.

"It will be necessary to travel light. I don't intend taking much. I've found a couple of sleeping-bags and an old knapsack lying around here. I've already done some packing. I suppose you'll need your ration book, but the less encumbrances the better." It appeared definite that he intended to go.

Footsteps once more sounded on the cobbles outside but, mercifully, they passed on by.

"Look," he continued. "For all I know the bloody coppers are watching this place, waiting to catch me go out. Why don't you go back to the hospital for anything you really need and at the same time do a bit of a recce to find out if anyone's waiting at the entrance to the mews. If you don't come back after five minutes, I'll assume the coast is clear and I'll push off to Euston. Then you could meet me there under the clock as soon as possible."

"Why Euston?"

"Why anywhere? I rather fancy Scotland. and I've got a cousin who's a crofter somewhere in the Moidart area. Never kept up with him. Bit of a recluse, I believe, although we were quite close as kids. He had polio when he was about sixteen. I suppose that's what kept him out of the war. Might look him up. If you're prepared to rough it we'll get along somehow. Maybe Colin could do with a bit of help."

Her panic had subsided now. She knew she would do as he wished, that she was, in fact, powerless to do otherwise. Besides, what was there left for her? She was under no illusions that her ability to attract the opposite sex was fading, that Michael Naresby could well be the last man with whom she might be able to form a close physical relationship, that she lacked the strength of character to deal with a returning estranged and reproachful husband. She therefore remained patiently waiting while Michael packed his final requirements for the journey.

Apart from the sound of her own footsteps, it was very quiet as she walked through the mews. Here and there a small chink of light showed, something which would have been unheard of until now. But the war on the home front was definitely 'running down'. A dim-out had supplanted the black-out. She moved slowly, not wishing to attract attention. There appeared to be no lurking figures as she turned into the street. Once again, she was reminded of the past, of how, once upon a time, she herself had been watched by Harvey's detectives. It occurred to her in some dim subconscious way that she had been running from something or somebody most of her life.

Collecting up her things into a small suitcase at the nurses' home was easier than she had anticipated. It was still only eight-thirty p.m. and the majority of nurses, having finished supper, were either out or in the common room. She was therefore able to slip away quietly. Well before ten and with infinite relief, she caught sight of Michael Naresby's figure, bedecked with small accoutrements, a little like a Christmas tree, waiting as pre-arranged under the clock at Euston. He had evidently had enough faith in her not to think she would let him down, for he told her at once that, although they would have to sit up, he had bought two tickets on the overnight express to Glasgow.

The journey was bleak, cold and exhausting. On nearing Carlisle Rose felt that, but for the flasks of whisky which Michael kept producing, she would like to have got out of the train and headed back to London. But the realisation that she was almost certain to have been missed by now, that the step she had taken was irrevocable and that she was infinitely weary, finally made her lay a head on his shoulder, where she fell into a broken sleep, troubled by dreams of empty flasks and being chased by the Law across Scottish moors.

Although Michael had originally suggested hitch-hiking north after Glasgow, she was thankful when he decided that they should take another train as far as Lochailort. It was also comforting to find that he seemed to have several thick bundles of bank notes on him with which he now paid for more tickets.

"I reckon it's important to spend a bit now," he remarked, "so as to put as much distance between us and London as soon as possible. When we get to Moidart it'll be time enough to cut down."

"But will your cousin put us up? I mean, what will he say when you suddenly descend on him? Especially with a female companion. It's all so . . . chancy."

"Of course it's chancy. All life's chancy. Haven't you learnt that?" He was brusque, almost rude. "But we'll just have to take pot luck, *literally*. If Colin doesn't want or isn't able to offer us a meal or let us help him in return for some keep, well, then we'll have to think again. I told you it wouldn't be a bed of roses, Rose. That's a good one, isn't it?" He gave a short laugh. "I'm not expecting a five-star hotel and you mustn't either. More like a hayloft, I shouldn't wonder. But I haven't been an army officer for nothing. What do you think we were all trained for in the build-up to D-Day? *Survival*. Knowing how to cope. Living off the land. *And* in a foreign country. Ye gods, we're still in the British Isles, Rose, even if the Scottish accent is a bit difficult to take. For God's sake, can't you look on this as bit of an adventure, a joint enterprise?"

The train to Lochailort went far more slowly. They arrived late that evening. She could hardly believe it was only twenty-four hours since they had left Euston.

"Someone should be able to direct us to Colin's place tomorrow," Michael said, as they alighted on the platform. "We'll ask at the post office. Right now, we'd better look for somewhere to sleep."

She followed him dumbly, blindly, as, with the aid of a torch, he led her, miraculously, to a disused barn. And there, huddled together in sleeping bags, Rose St Clair had her first taste of sleeping rough.

30

They called Michael's cousin "Crusoe" in the small village to which the travellers were eventually directed—Crusoe Chadwick. Although no one knew him well, everyone seemed to know *of* him. He was "the silent chap", "crazy as a coot", "a queer hawk". But all agreed that he was a master mariner when it came to handling a boat.

It appeared that he was the sole inhabitant of a tiny island, one and half miles wide by two long and exactly one mile off the coast. He had been living there quite alone since the mid thirties, raising sheep and a few red deer, keeping chickens and, on the leeward side of the island, planting spruce and conifers. Inch by grudging inch he had rolled back a barren wilderness to create a little self-contained farm where with the initial help of Hamish McIntyre, a local builder, he had built a small but sturdy whitewashed stone house in which he had been prevailed upon by Hamish to have a telephone installed. Few people in the neighbourhood had ever seen the inside of Crusoe's home, except Hamish and the dealers who occasionally visited the island to buy the kind of quality sheep its owner reared. Once a week he came to the mainland to sell eggs and replenish his stores although, when gales lashed the area, he was marooned for weeks on end.

"We used to worry about him," Hamish's wife said, "but then we realised he dinna like that. So we let him be."

"Is there anyone who would pilot us across?" Michael asked. "I'm a relative," he added, by way of explaining their wish to visit him.

She looked doubtful, even a little scared. "Och, no. That wuidna do at all, I'm thinking, even if you are his kin. Besides, there's a pretty strong north-westerly blowin'. Ye cuid telephone, I suppose. But it might be best to wait till he next comes on over."

"When will that be?"

"Friday. If the seas calm down. But ye never know. Best just to bide a wee. Ye'll have nowhere to stop the whiles?"

"No."

"Och, well . . . " She began looking even more doubtful, her eyes taking in their dishevelled appearance, the lack of a wedding ring on Rose's hand. To the latter's astonishment, she then heard Michael say, calmly and with what seemed like perfect truthfulness, "My sister and I have been recently bombed out, you see. Our house in London caught one of the last of Hitler's rockets."

"Och, ye puir things." Mrs McIntyre's manner completely changed. "No wonder ye're looking for a little peace and quiet. Well, now. I daresay my brother-in-law, Jock Fraser, who owns the Stag down by the jetty, wuid put you up the whiles. He doesn't usually let rooms but in your case, I'm sure he'd make an exception."

The thought of a bed and a possible bath temporarily took away Rose's feeling of embarrassment—and, if she were honest, reluctant admiration—for Michael's quick-thinking duplicity; although, once alone in bed that night, a certain fear took hold of her. Deep down, it confirmed her sense of having thrown in her lot with a "bad 'un", even if she herself had much to answer for. She was aware that for the sake of a passionate desire to be with one man and an equally passionate desire not to have to face another, she had made her worst mistake, that she was slipping, going under, her whole identity at risk. Michael had even conferred an assumed surname on them both.

The door of her room opened so slowly that she did not hear it, only the sound of a soft footstep as Michael reached the side of her bed.

"Rose!" He lifted the covers and slipped in beside her. "I think we should take the opportunity, don't you? I mean, life, as you said, is a bit chancy at the moment. I'm sure our good host hasn't the slightest suspicion that our relationship is not what I said it was."

She responded instantly to his embraces. He had always been able to make her feel alive as soon as he touched her. Tonight, he restored the identity which had earlier threatened to desert her. She opened her arms and drew him closer. "Hardly the act of a sister," he murmured, with a quiet laugh, as they began to make love.

When Friday came the wind had dropped and the sea was relatively calm, but there was no sign of Colin Chadwick. From a window in the bar at the Stag it was possible to see across to the island and to keep a watch for the Crusoe clipper, as his boat had been affectionately dubbed.

"That's odd," Jock remarked, when it got to midday. "I've never known him not put out to sea in weather like this. He's usually here well by now. Maybe I'll give him a ring."

But after three attempts to contact Colin, there was still no answer.

"Mebbe we shuid find out what's goin' on." Jock said, finally hanging up. He called to his wife to take over the bar. "Y'uid like to come with me, I dare say. I've got an old motor-boat down by the jetty."

"Thank you. I think we'd like to do that very much."

The journey did not take them long. In less than twenty minutes they were scrambling up the steps of what passed for the island's harbour, while Jock Fraser secured his boat along-side Colin's.

They found his house empty but immaculate. It was evident that Michael's cousin lived in perfect shipshape fashion. There were signs that the kitchen had been used that morning, but only because a dishcloth and tea-towel were slightly damp.

"What was that?" It was Rose who heard the barking first. They listened. From the direction of the cliffs to the south west there came the faint but unmistakable sound of a dog—a dog who was fearful, excited, demanding attention.

The three of them began running then, stumbling over the springy but uneven turf. On reaching higher ground they saw a tractor, a collie beside it and a rope extending from the middle of the machine and running taut over the edge of the cliff.

"Och, he'll have gone after a sheep, I reckon," Jock shouted, as he ran even faster.

Within seconds they were all three staring down to where Colin Chadwick lay, doubled up on a narrow ledge, the body of a dead sheep caught by a small boulder a little way below him.

"I'll go." To his credit, Michael wasted no time in now taking the initiative. There was another coil of rope on the tractor seat and it was agreed that Jock should move the machine so that it faced inland. Michael then tied one end of the rope around the back axle and the other round himself. Gingerly, he edged himself over the side of the cliff, his legs dangling perilously near to his cousin's head. Once on the ledge beside him he managed, with an amazing show of strength and dexterity, to gather up Colin's body and encircle it with an extension of the same rope which held him. Rose, kneeling down, now yelled to Jock in the cab's driving seat to start moving and, slowly but surely, Michael and Colin were winched up until their bodies lay on top of the cliff, the one panting and exhausted, the other inert and seemingly lifeless, to which the nurse in Rose now ministered with remarkable efficiency.

"Is he dead?" Jock came and stood beside them.

"No. But pretty nearly." With her hand still on Colin's pulse, she continued quickly, "Hospital. We must get him to hospital. Could you go down to the house and telephone for an ambulance and see if there's anything we could use as a stretcher and perhaps a tea-towel or two and a small piece of wood that would make a splint."

In no time at all it seemed as if Jock returned with the necessary requirements. Then, having made Colin as comfortable as possible and with Michael revived, the three of them were able to transport his cousin down to his makeshift harbour.

"I reckon it wuid be best to take Crusoe's own boat," Jock said. "It's bigger. I've never handled it before but it shouldn't be all that difficult."

A little crowd had gathered on the mainland to greet them on arrival, including an empty ambulance which had miraculously been travelling in the vicinity. Had the circumstances been different, Rose would have asked to go with her patient. Now, she hung back. She knew full well that questions would be asked at the hospital, awkward questions such as Colin's next-of-kin and why she had become involved in his accident. It was important that she and Michael maintained anonymity. It was one thing to take on the name of Ford and present themselves as brother and sister for the benefit of the local inhabitants, but quite another to lay themselves open to any kind of official inquisition. She was grateful when, quite suddenly, the voice of Hamish McIntyre spoke up, offering to accompany the injured man.

For a few moments, as they watched the ambulance winding its way up the steep hill from the jetty, there was complete silence. Then Jock Fraser turnd to Michael and said, "There's livestock over there. Feeding to be done. A house-cow needs milking. We canna let them be."

"No. I understand." Michael now turned to Rose. "Coming?"

"Of course."

With that streak of intrepidity in both of them which occasionally superseded the less commendable and cowardly side of their characters, Rose St Clair and Michael Naresby now headed back to Crusoe's island.

31

There followed a surprisingly calm and rewarding time for the temporary caretakers of Crusoe's island. Both of them had a good basic understanding of the land and its requirements. Both, now that their creature comforts, particularly alcohol, were in short supply, became fitter and therefore in many ways happier. Except for the constant awareness that they were only in their present position by default, that the Law, in one form or another, might catch up with them at any minute, or the island's owner return and ask them to leave, they could easily have settled for this kind of simple country existence. Often, it came to Rose that it was the life she was meant to lead, that all the desperate imprudent years since she had left the safety of her Norfolk upbringing had been but a chimera, something which had happened to somebody else over which she had had no control. The beauty of this part of the Scottish coast captivated her. Battling with the elements, in tune with the wildness and the privacy, satisfied some need in her. She did not think she could ever return to an indoor life again.

V.E. Day and the end of the war in Europe seemed to pass her by. Having, quite by accident, caught the announcement on the wireless of Germany's final capitulation, she simply went out to attend to one of the various tasks which had automatically come her way and which seemed far more important. In any case, the news which concerned her most was that about Colin, which Jock Fraser or Hamish McIntyre relayed by telephone each week after visiting the hospital where he had lain in a coma ever since the accident.

One Sunday evening towards the end of May she caught sight of Jock's boat approaching and walked down to the harbour, watching it come closer, dipping and rising on a gentle swell. Having had no telephone call that day, she felt she already knew what he had come to tell them. Nor was she wrong in her surmise. Colin Chadwick had died the previous night.

Rose had occasionally tried to discuss with Michael what they could or should do should such an eventuality come to pass, although she was invariably met with short non-committal replies. When she told him of his cousin's death, she saw the look of fear come into his eyes that she had first witnessed when the doodle-bugs had been at their worst. She realised, of course, that he was still, to all intents and purposes, on the run. Indeed, they both were. But she had no idea as to the extent of his criminal activities. Their peaceful life on the island had all but lulled her into a false sense of security. Whenever unwelcome thoughts had intruded she had been able to quell them by keeping busy. If, very occasionally, such worries woke her at night, she comforted herself by thinking the end of the war, with all its attendant chaos and complexities, had probably meant that any hounding of either Michael or herself had fallen by the way.

Yet she knew that even if neither of them had been wanted people, it was obvious Colin's death would mean that they could not remain where they were. They had no right whatsoever to be occupying Crusoe's island. Presumably a will would be found, a solicitor would appear. Some little man wearing a black coat and pinstripe trousers, reminiscent of Ernest MacKenzie who had come to see her after Harvey's death, would turn up, most likely ferried across from the mainland by Jock. He would ask awkward questions. The property would be sold. But what would happen to the livestock while all that came about? She had come to love the cow she had learnt to milk—albeit now dry—whom she had christened Mirabelle, the black-faced sheep who always seemed to seek her out, the collie named Tina who now slept in her and Michael's bedroom.

"I shall have to go to Glasgow," he said to her one morning, after receiving a telephone call. "Apparently there have been enquiries made on the mainland, people getting on to Hamish and Jock. My name came up, obviously—that is, the name of Ford. A firm called Haswell and Petter want to see me."

"Oh. When will you go?"

He shrugged. He was distinctly uneasy. "Next week,

perhaps. I don't see why I should hurry. Solicitors are notorious for dragging their feet. After all, it's quite a while since Colin died."

"Yes. Did he have no one, do you think? I mean, some next-of-kin. It seemed so sad that Hamish was named simply because he went with him to the hospital."

"Search me. I've never kept up with any of the family. Colin was a loner. Like me."

He became increasingly moody in the days which followed. It reminded her all too plainly of his behaviour in London. When, over a week later, he received a letter from Glasgow, he flew into a rage and she did not see him again until evening.

Slightly penitent, he said to her. "I'll ring those damned solicitors tomorrow and fix an appointment. Get it over with. Perhaps you could take me over to the mainland when the time comes. I don't like to leave you without means of transport. Jock can bring me back."

"As you will." She knew she had become rather good at handling the Crusoe clipper, something on which not only Michael but also Hamish and Jock complimented her. "How long will you be gone?" she continued.

"I can't do it in a day," was all he replied.

Later that night she came across him looking for one of the sleeping-bags which they had brought with them on their initial journey. "Not a lot of cash left," he said, shortly. "I know we've been able to subsidise ourselves with the egg money and selling those lambs, but . . . well . . . that doesn't exactly run to a four-star hotel. I might have to doss down somewhere. You don't mind being alone here, do you?"

"No."

Yet, after he had gone, she realised that she did mind. She had not expected such a traumatic reaction to complete solitude. She was aware that basically she was more self-sufficient than Michael, that she was practical and her nurse's training stood her in good stead. But without male companion-ship she was lost. It was somehow imperative for her to have a man around. She longed for the following evening when he had said he would return.

She went and sat with Tina on the slope above the harbour

at about six o'clock, scanning the mainland through a pair of binoculars which they had found in the house. The distant shore was golden, the sky still azure blue. A poem of Yeats which she had learnt at school, and scarcely since thought about, came suddenly into her mind: *Light of evening, Lissadell* . . . The beauty all around seemed almost too perfect. A feeling of great sadness came over her, for she sensed that her days on the island were numbered. Absently, she fondled the collie, then picked up the binoculars once again, hoping for signs of Michael's return.

She waited while the shadows lengthened and a mist obscured the far shore. Then she went back to the house and began shutting up the hens, watering the small garden she had tended, casting a look at Mirabelle in the paddock, tapping the barometer and noting that it had made a remarkable drop since morning. Still hoping that Michael would appear, she kept going outside, walking down to the harbour in the twilight, with Tina at her heels. She did not feel like eating. All she did feel was a sense of unease which increased as the hours went by.

A wind got up about ten o'clock. She knew that Jock was perfectly capable of handling a boat at night but she hoped Michael would stop with their friend, with whom he had made an arrangement to fetch him from the station given prior warning by telephone. She felt justified, now, in giving Jock a call herself.

"Nerry a word," came the answer. "He'll be spending another night in Glasgow, I reckon. The last train to Lochailart wuid have come and gone by now."

She put down the receiver. Something had gone wrong. Very wrong. She knew that for a certainty. For one thing the weekend was upon them. No solicitors worked on Saturdays and Sundays. And why hadn't Michael telephoned her himself? It was the least he could have done.

She hardly slept that night, nor the following two. On Monday morning a man called Tanner rang her from Haswell and Petter's enquiring as to the whereabouts of Mr Michael Ford, whom they had been expecting the previous Thursday but who had failed to keep his appointment. When she explained that, as far as she knew, he was in Glasgow for the express purpose of such a meeting, the voice on the other end of the line said, curtly, "Well, if you are in contact with him, perhaps you would be kind enough to let us know. Meanwhile, I will speak to my colleague about the situation."

She began to shake then. Dear God, Michael had been gone five days. And he had never reached Haswell and Petter. He probably never intended to. She saw it all now. The desire for her to keep the boat, the sleeping-bag, the raiding of her small stock of tins "in case of emergencies", as he had put it. Michael had vamoosed, ducked out. It was D-Day all over again, or the night the police called at the mews. He lived to a pattern. When things went wrong, he ran. He had probably been far more involved in the black market than she had ever suspected. He would have known that, once confronted by solicitors, the fact that he had adopted an assumed name would be almost certain to come out, that prison bars were closing in on him.

Miserably, she waited three more days, wrestling with the problem of what she should do. A further call from Haswells' decided the matter for her. She searched out the second sleeping-bag, unearthed an old haversack, packed into it as many requirements as she was able and made a final inspection of the livestock. Then, in the early hours of the following morning, she set out with Tina for the mainland.

Here, she moored the Crusoe clipper and left inside it a note addressed jointly to Jock and Hamish, explaining that it was necessary for her to go away herself for a while and asking them if, in the goodness of their hearts, they could possibly make regular trips to the island to see to the animals. She ended by giving them the address and telephone number of Haswell and Petter, to whom she recommended them to refer for temporary instructions.

At two thirty she started walking. By nine o'clock that morning she and Tina were on the train for Glasgow.

32

A heavily burdened woman and a dog walking the streets of Glasgow at that time might not, in the ordinary way, have attracted much attention. In keeping with many another city, it was teeming with G.I.s and G.I. brides still waiting for a passage back to the States. Moreover, election fever was sweeping the country and Rose found her arrival had coincided with Winston Churchill's, now towards the end of what was to prove his unavailing tour of the provinces. In the mean, crowded, blitzed streets, there were countless people who looked as if they might have been sleeping rough and Rose felt that she could easily have maintained complete anonymity, but for one problem: Tina.

She knew that the collie was a young one, but she had never taken into account that Tina had probably never before been in a town and that she had only experienced life on a lonely island, with Colin Chadwick as her sole companion. Before they even stepped outside the station, the dog began to shake. Then she sat down and refused to move. All attempts at pulling or persuasion were useless. Rose, lacking sleep and having no clear idea exactly why she had come to Glasgow—except that in some illogical hopeless way she wondered whether she might run into Michael—now sat down herself in the nearest doorway, put one arm round the terrified animal, rested her head on her knees—and wept.

She was utterly astonished when she felt something being pressed into her other hand. Looking up, she encountered the kind concerned eyes of an American corporal, uncannily reminiscent of Elmer Burke. Then, just as suddenly, he was gone, leaving her staring, with a mixture of horror and fascination, at the pound note she was still holding. When, half an hour later, the same thing happened again, except that this time the donor was merely a private, she realised that she was being taken for what she had virtually become: a beggar.

Secreting the money in a small purse which she had attached to a belt worn close to her person, she got up and made another attempt to cross to the other side of the road, where she had seen the welcoming sign of a British Restaurant. She was feeling hungry now and suspected the dog must be as well. She knew that those in charge of such establishments would probably be kindly disposed towards Tina for, throughout the war, it had always seemed as if food shops and cafés had tended to give extra titbits to animals rather than humans. She recalled how the butcher at Kinton would alway slip her a little extra meat for Sweep, which often proved far superior to any of the rations in the St Clair household.

With tremendous coaxing, she at last managed to get the collie half way across the busy thoroughfare, where they became marooned on a small concrete island. Then the inevitable happened. Tina panicked, slipped her collar and darted under a passing jeep. With a screech of brakes, the driver drew up and came running back, by which time Rose, with all traffic halted around her, had run forward and was kneeling down, cradling the collie's head in her lap.

"I am so vurry sorry."

This time she found herself looking up into the shocked face of an American colonel.

"It's not your fault. There was nothing you could have done. The dog went berserk."

"Is it . . . dead?"

"Yes."

"May I drive you both home?"

"No . . . thank you. That is, I should be very grateful if you could . . . take Tina somewhere to be buried."

"Sure." He hesitated. "But are you certain you won't come too?"

"Quite certain. I'd just like to think the dog's body was properly . . . attended to. A vet, perhaps," she added, uncertainly, although where and how the man was going to find one in the centre of Glasgow, she had no idea.

"Sure," he said again, as he gathered Tina into his arms, ignoring the blood which spattered on to his immaculate uniform. "It's the least I can do," he continued, as he carried

the lifeless bundle into the back of the jeep. Then he turned to
Rose and, for the third time that morning, she found herself
being offered money. "Please," he said, "don't get me wrong.
I know nothing I can do can compensate for what has just
happened. I suppose you could say that this is a purely selfish
gesture. But it would help me tremendously if you would
accept it."

She knew that he had taken in her unkempt down-and-out
appearance. Yet she also knew that he was genuinely upset
and out to do his best in the unfortunate circumstances. It
seemed churlish to refuse. Besides, the practical side of her
realised that she was hardly in a position to adopt too much
pride. But, sadly, she was only too well aware that his offer
and attentiveness were very different from the kind she had
been accustomed to experiencing in days gone by, when the
opposite sex made overtures for quite another reason. That
particular asset which she had once possessed no longer
applied. She was not a woman any man would look at twice.
All that had happened on this particular morning had shown
her, as nothing else might have done, that she was a drop-out
in society: a female itinerant old before her time, worn, tired
and dishevelled. Almost involuntarily, she accepted the notes
being handed to her, although not before the jeep had disappeared from view did she find that she was the recipient of
fifty pounds. It seemed a fortune. She was quite unaware of
the extent of gratitude felt by every returning ex-serviceman
towards all and sundry, simply for being alive.

Distraught by the loss of Tina, Rose spent the next three
months in Glasgow, dossing down in bombed-out buildings,
on park benches, in the odd welfare centre and, occasionally,
if she could find one, paying for some kind of lodging where
she could take a bath. As Christmas approached and the cold
intensified—by which time she had long given up hope of ever
seeing Michael again—she decided to move south. She had
purchased a small road map and, armed with this, she set out,
sometimes walking, sometimes hitch-hiking, sometimes
making a short journey by bus or train. At one point, with a
shock, she found that she was not far from Kinton. She looked
across to the Pennines towering in the distance. She wondered

what had happened to her parents-in-law, to George Lorrimer and most of all to John. Was he still looking for her or had he given up hope? Guiltily, she realised that he would be unable to marry again for many years until she could be presumed dead.

In the summer of 1946 she reached London. She was twenty-nine. She could have been fifty. She had become withdrawn now, speaking as little as possible to those she had come across on her marathon journey. With no home, no male companion, no dog, the loss of identity which had often threatened to overwhelm her became acute. Once back among her former haunts, she decided, as far as the rest of the world was concerned, to make it complete. Rose St Clair, née Delafield, vagrant of no fixed address, threw her ration book over Westminster Bridge. It was true that owing to her peripatetic existence, she had more or less managed to do without it for the last twelve months. Now, where she was more likely to be challenged by authority, she desired that nothing about her should give a clue to her past. If forced to answer questions, she would pretend confusion due to having been a victim of bombing.

For a while, incredibly, she escaped notice. Then, one morning after spending the night in Hyde Park, a policeman stopped and asked where she came from. Disturbed by the unsatisfactory monosyllabic response, he took her along to Savile Row police station. Baffled, the officer in charge sent her to the Middlesex Hospital. Here, she was found to be totally unco-operative but physically fit. Eventually, she was given a new ration book—under the name of her late aunt, Belle Jackson, which it had suddenly occurred to her to use—and discharged on the understanding that she should report each night to one of the new social centres which were springing up, mostly in the east end.

With the nights drawing in, Rose at first made no objection, although she spoke to no one and each day gravitated back to central London where she would sit, usually outside a food shop from which, sooner or later, someone would be sure to come out and hand her a bun or some fruit which would otherwise have gone bad. She was not, as such, breaking any law. She was not making a nuisance of herself or obstructing the

course of justice. Often, the heap of rags in some corner went
unnoticed by passers-by, as it blended in with the overall
drabness of post-war London. If, at any time, a policeman
asked her to move on, she shuffled off quietly. Members of the
force began to think of her as a kind of mascot. They called
her Belle and treated her kindly and sympathetically. When,
for some reason, her mood took her away from the Hyde Park
area for a while, they would remark on her absence, hoping all
was well with her.

For there were times when she felt an irresistible urge to go
back to Hampstead, where she discovered that three new
houses were being built on the site of Elena's old one. She
would sit, for hours on end, watching the men at work, noting
the obviously get-rich-quick entrepreneur who appeared now
and then to inspect the ugly monstrosities being erected with
shoddy, inadequate materials, devoid of all beauty or design.
Once, she actually broke her self-imposed silence by asking
one of the builders whether they had found a picture while
digging the foundations. He looked at her blankly and shook
his head. As she went back and squatted down on the other
side of the road, she heard him remark to one of his mates,
"Funny how she 'aunts this spot. Bit of a nut-case, I suppose,
poor old soul."

Sometimes she went to look at the homes she had shared
with Harvey and with Stephen and the mews from which she
and Michael had fled to Scotland. Once or twice she almost
brought herself to knock on the door, in the hopes that it was
still inhabited by Michael's friend and that he might know of
his whereabouts. Then recalling the words of the workman in
Hampstead, she desisted. She was a "poor old soul", a travesty
of the woman Michael had once known.

Many was the time, at night, as she lay in the doss-house,
when she would start going back over the years which had
brought her to her present state. Although she pretended to
confusion, her mind was perfectly clear. Little bright hurting—
and occasionally joyful—memories came flooding back. She
thought of the good-looking aesthetic man who had been her
father, could see his photograph on her dressing-table at
Wilcot until she had banished it to a drawer once Harvey had

begun making his nocturnal visits to the tower suite. She could recall her first Christmas spent under his roof and how Carl Scholtc had said, "Don't move," when he had caught sight of her in the black velvet dress, because he had known instantly that this was a portrait he had to paint. She relived, almost tangibly, the summer of the coronation, the warm moonlit night on the forecourt when Stephen had first kissed her—followed by Harvey's increasing jealousy and suspicion, his ultimate suicide and the agony of the inquest.

Then there had been the happy time with Stephen, particularly the weeks spent in the Loire valley. Why hadn't their relationship lasted? What exactly went wrong? Would it have been different if they had married? She could not blame the war, although it had certainly come between them and altered both their lives. She wondered what had become of her third lover, Henry Somerville, and whether he had survived the holocaust.

As for John and the baby . . . this was where her thoughts were invariably brought up short. It was better to draw a veil over her marriage and her time at Kinton and her affair with George Lorrimer. It was far easier to pass on to the years she had spent doing a full nurse's training. At least she had made an effort over that, even if it included destroying the hopes and illusions of one poor G.I. and playing the field with many others.

Lastly, she would come to Michael: weak, sometimes brutal but, of all her lovers, the most physically attractive and magnetic. She would never know now what had happened to him, any more than she would know about her husband or any of the people who had come into and gone out of her life in such kaleidoscope fashion. They seemed on the other side of some invisible barrier, characters in another world from which she had abdicated. No one would believe her story, even if she tried to tell it: that she was once, in 1936, the talk of London's artistic circles after *Portrait of Rose* had been hung in that year's Summer Exhibition at the Royal Academy. Should she ever, by the remotest chance, come across the picture, how could she possibly claim to be the sitter?

33

In the early 1950s, Susan Fanshawe, née Buckley, sat on the sitting-room floor of a terraced house near Hyde Park Corner, playing with her two small children, Kate and Martin. She was a pretty young matron, happily married to a paediatrician working at Great Ormond Street Hospital. Theirs was by no means a large or luxurious home and was still in need of considerable repair, having suffered indirect damage through VIs and V2s dropped in the vicinity in the spring of 1945; but it had the advantage of a small secluded garden at the back and a good nursery school which had just opened up round the corner.

The Fanshawes knew that any improvements would take time, not only because builders and building materials were still in short supply, but also because they possessed little money to spare. They had met towards the end of the war, when Dick Fanshawe was an M.O. attached to a Royal Artillery Regiment on Salisbury Plain and Susan had been a company commander in a nearby A.T.S. unit stationed at Tidworth.

Their courtship and marriage had been conducted on conventional, somewhat old-fashioned lines, which might have been expected from two such individuals: one the younger son of a country doctor, the other the only daughter of James Buckley, a much-respected tenant farmer in the west country. Sadly, he had never lived to fulfil two ambitions: to see the annihilation of Hitler and the Nazis, and his beloved daughter married. In keeping with the custom of many a man in a similar position, he had left the bulk of his estate—apart from a few minor legacies—outright to his wife, knowing that she, in turn, would be sure to pass it on to Susan. Not for him the kind of will which involved trusts and by-passing his widow, so that she only received a life interest. To him, such an arrangement would have been insulting to his dearest companion of so many years. Therefore Anne Buckley now lived comfortably in Larcombe Cottage, which she had been able to buy outright from Sir Reginald Farquharson, who had previously let it to service personnel at Southern Command, such as Major Henry Somerville. Thanks to many local contacts and her late husband's fine reputation, assistance in doing up and expanding her new home had come from many sources so that, unlike her daughter in London, Anne had relatively quickly been able to achieve a most desirable residence for her retirement.

Every so often she came to London and stayed with Susan and Dick and, at times such as Christmas or Easter, they visited her. She doted on the little boy and girl they had produced and kept in constant touch. It was a happy, uncomplicated and mutually rewarding state of affairs.

After James Buckley's death, Anne had maintained her subscription to *Country Life* and, one day early in 1951, she opened the magazine to be confronted by a face she recollected well. It was that of a young woman whose portrait was up for sale in a certain art gallery in George Street, W.1.

Knowing how much Rose Delafield had once meant to her daughter and also feeling that Susan had long grown out of her youthful infatuation—one which she herself had deplored—she tore out the relevant page and posted it on to her with "Whatever happened to Rose?" scrawled across the top.

It arrived on a morning when Susan happened to have a little daily help. Leaving the children in her care for an hour or so, she went off immediately to the Berliss Gallery. It was not quite the kind of place she expected, as it was crowded with *objets d'art*, bric-à-brac, small ornate tables and china figurines. But the young man in charge was courteous in the extreme and took her straight across to the wall, where *Portrait of Rose* hung in all its glory.

Susan stood looking at it. The years rolled back. This was the woman she had so admired and wanted to emulate. She could understand at once why the picture had caused such a sensation at the time. Carl Scholte had genius. Today, over fifteen years later, Rose seemed to be here, with her in the gallery, so alive that she might have stepped out of the frame.

There was the shining auburn hair, the large eyes, the full slightly parted lips, the half innocent yet subtly aware expression which Susan, in maturity, recognised for what it was: sex appeal. She herself knew that however much she was loved by her husband, she had never had the kind of attraction for men which Rose had appeared to exude unconsciously.

She moved forward a little to examine the details, whereupon the salesman said, quickly, "It was evidently damaged at some time. Probably in the war. The bottom left-hand corner has been restored, but with great expertise, as you will have noted. There is no doubt it is an original Scholte, although the signature was, unfortunately, obliterated."

"Yes. I wasn't doubting its authenticity." She stepped back again. "How did you come by it?"

The young man spread his hands. "My boss, Mr Berliss, who owns the gallery. . . He goes to many sales, you understand, all over the country. There is nothing he does not know about pictures. But he came across this one when the contents of a second-hand shop were being sold because the owner had died. Naturally, he called in other experts to examine this latest discovery. Such a very beautiful young lady, is she not?"

"Yes. Very beautiful." Sadly, Susan realised that there would be no hope of tracing Rose through her portrait.

"You are perhaps acquainted with the work of this particular painter?" He was obviously pleased and intrigued by her interest.

"I . . . happened to know him slightly." Something warned her not to become too enthusiastic, in view of what was forming in her mind.

"Really? How fortunate. A great man. A great artist."

"How much. . .?" she asked, slowly, "are you asking for the portrait?"

"A thousand."

"*A thousand?*"

"Yes, madam. But for the damage it would be double."

She thought of the money Dick had saved up for the new roof, her own little deposit account at the bank to which she was able to add now and then, thanks to her mother often passing over a dividend from one of her investments. She remembered Grandmother Buckley's old-fashioned amethyst pendant which she knew she would never wear, yet had never liked to sell. How could she ever bring herself to tell her husband she had committed an act that was so totally out of keeping with her usual sensible self? But she knew it would be no good telling him beforehand and expecting his acquiescence and blessing. She would have to buy the picture and then face the consequences.

She sensed that the young man was standing expectantly beside her, not quite knowing whether to speak or not to speak, praying that he had made a sale. She wondered whether to offer a lower sum. But she was not used to bargaining. There seemed something faintly distasteful about haggling over Rose. And she wanted the picture more than she could possibly explain. When she told him she would take it, she felt as if the words were being put into her mouth by somebody else.

"I will let you have a deposit now and the balance of the money on Monday. I live in central London. Would you be able to deliver the portrait later that week?"

"*Mais oui, madame.*" In his relief and excitement he had broken into French. "I am delighted that you have decided to buy it. I am sure you will not be disappointed. I feel you were meant to have it, that you have . . . how shall I put it . . . fallen in love with the sitter."

She made her way home, half dazed by what she had done, his last words repeating themselves over and over in her mind. She supposed she *had* fallen in love with Rose a long time ago, back in 1935 or '36. She could never remember ever feeling the same way about anyone else, not even Dick. And it had not seemed just a youthful crush, as the girls at school used to refer to such a condition. It had lasted. Could it be that she was unnatural? She could not bring herself to use the word lesbian. Heaven forbid! She was a much-loved and loving wife and mother, leading a most satisfactory respectable life, which she would not wish to change for anything else in the world. Yet she had parted with a good portion of the family savings for a portrait of Rose, hadn't she? And she would have given even more to have known what had happened to her.

Many was the time when she had tried to find out. Once she had even advertised in the personal column of *The Times*. At the end of the war she had written to John St Clair and he had come to London to meet her in the hopes that, between them, they might be able to light on some clue as to his wife's disappearance. He still kept in touch with Susan, writing from time to time from a farm a hundred miles away from Kinton where, not having any capital, he had started by being a pupil and was gradually working his way up to a managerial position. He had mentioned that he had hoped a farmer by the name of George Lorrimer, who lived in his home village and whom he had known all his life, might have taken him on, but Mr Lorrimer had been unable to help in this way. Apparently his wife had suffered continual ill-health and he had intimated that he was thinking of retiring before long, in order to devote more time to her. John had obviously been disappointed that he had not found a position nearer to Kinton, because his mother had died and, although his aunt still lived at the rectory, he felt his father needed more moral support, having spent many years caring for a senile wife.

Susan felt intensely sorry for John. It occurred to her now that it was he rather than she who should be in possession of Rose's portrait. Yet, even if he could have afforded it—which he most definitely could not—she comforted herself by reflecting that there were at least two good reasons why this would hardly be appropriate. One was that she had an idea that Rose had never told John very much about her past life. A picture like this would be bound to start him guessing. The other was that he had, as yet, no place of his own in which to hang it and, as for its gracing the walls of Kinton rectory, this, somehow, seemed quite out of the question.

But she could hardly wait to get it hung in her own home. It was due to arrive on the morning of the following Thursday, presumably after her final cheque had been presented and safely cleared. It was fortunate that she happened to have a carpenter coming to do some minor repairs that week and he had promised to put it up for her. When the time came he seemed to become infected by her own enthusiasm. Nothing was too much trouble. He spent almost an hour holding it above the fireplace in the sitting-room, raising or lowering it an inch or so until she was satisfied that they had got the position absolutely right. At last they both stood back, mutually admiring Rose.

"Fair corker, ain't she?" he remarked, in a strong cockney voice.

Susan smiled. 'Corker' was not quite the word she would have chosen to describe Rose, but it was plain the little carpenter had got the sitter's message all right.

"Bet the guv'nor likes it, don't 'e?" he went on.

For the first time since the portrait's arrival, Susan was assailed by apprehension.

"He hasn't actually seen it yet."

"Not seen it?" The man gave her a sideways look. "Bin 'anded down, 'as it? Heirloom, like?"

"Not . . . exactly. It's just someone I used to know."

"Ah, well. I'd best be gettin' on wi' them floorboards." He went away. She could tell he was distinctly nonplussed.

Dick Fanshawe was tired when he arrived home at seven thirty. There had been two particularly harrowing cases admitted to the ward where he worked that day, but he gave Susan his customary kiss, enquired after his children and sent up, as usual, a little silent prayer that all was well with his own family. As he sat down to a meal in the kitchen, he also thanked God for such a capable wife and mother, who never talked too much at the end of the day.

He did not notice the portrait when they first went into the sitting-room after supper. He had bought an evening paper and he simply sat reading it, while Susan picked up some needlework. Dick Fanshawe was not a man who took much interest in the arts. He was content to rely on his wife's judgment over the question of interior decoration and, so far, had been only too pleased to sit back and enjoy the pleasant ambience she created, with admirable thrift.

She had gone back to the kitchen to make hot drinks, which was their usual custom preparatory to retiring, when she heard him shout.

"Good God!"

Immediately, she came running back into the sitting-room.

"What the hell's that picture doing here?"

"I bought it," she answered, simply.

"You *bought* it!" He was standing up now, frowning and staring at it in utter astonishment. Then he turned to her, a mixture of bewilderment and belligerence on his face. "Why?" he asked.

"It's of someone I used to know. The girl I told you about who disappeared."

His frown deepened. "Who did you buy it from?"

"A gallery. In George Street."

She knew it had to come. "How much?" His eyes had narrowed. She had never seen him look quite like this before.

"A thousand."

"*A thousand!*" he repeated, rather as she had done to the young man in the Berliss Gallery.

There was a long silence. Then he said, "Have you gone mad, Susan?"

"No. I don't think so. I . . . well, I felt I just had to have it. Don't you see? It's Rose. She may have disappeared in the flesh but at least I've got her portrait."

"I think we should talk about this in the morning," was all he replied, coldly, as he stalked out of the door. That night, for the first time in their married life, they slept in separate rooms.

It was never quite the same for Susan and Dick Fanshawe after that. Although he forgave his wife and, to his credit, never actually asked her to sell the portrait, Rose seemed to come between them, looking down, teasingly, smiling, sometimes, Susan felt when at her most despondent, as if the sitter were trying to seduce Dick. One day she had suddenly come across her husband studying the picture with a curious expression, almost of fascination, on his face. Embarrassed, he had walked away. Many was the time when she regretted buying *Portrait of Rose* and was almost on the point of getting rid of it. For all she knew, it might have been worth much more now, because Carl Scholte's work was definitely having a revival. She noticed that his name was continually coming up in the press whenever there was an article on painting. She could contact Christies or Sothebys and then, perhaps, present her husband with a cheque for well over a thousand. But, with her hand on the telephone receiver, something always held her back.

Susan never knew—how could she—that the bundle of rags which so often occupied a corner outside the bakery near Shepherd Market, where she was accustomed to going for fruit and vegetables, was the woman she had long been seeking. Occasionally, she tossed a coin or two into the voluminous lap. But the old outsize peaked cap worn by the recipient precluded her seeing much of the face beneath. Susan's children, having once heard a policeman refer to the apparition as "Belle", would often stop and stand stock-still on catching sight of her, until their mother hustled them along telling them it was rude to stare.

In the new welfare state which had come into being since the end of the war, Susan thought it was totally wrong that any human being should have been allowed to sink to such depths of destitution as the beggar she frequently encountered. But, once back in her own home, she would forget about the sorry sight and look up at the picture hanging on her sitting-room wall: Rose Delafield, a young woman then in her prime. The portrait was much admired by the Fanshawes' visitors, many of whom complimented Susan on her artistic acumen. Even Dick, in time, came to realise that the family possessed an increasingly valuable asset.

"Mummy," little Kate said one day, after she had asked and been allowed to give Rose an apple on the way back from the market, "That old woman. I saw her eyes. Big ones, like in the picture you bought."

Susan smiled. She realised that it would be much easier for a toddler to get a better view of the face beneath the strange headgear.

"Do you think," the child persisted, "that Belle was ever pretty once upon a time?"

"I really don't know, darling," she answered, catching a tighter hold of the child's hand as they crossed the street.

But Rose knew, of course. Covertly, she watched them pass out of sight. It would have been nice, she felt, for Susan's little girl to have seen her portrait, to have explained that she and it were one and the same. But she was forgetting. Even a child's imagination would hardly stretch that far. She must not dwell in the past. She must remember that she was now Belle and had no desire to speak to old acquaintances, even those who passed her in the street.

For too long now she had maintained a vow of silence.